D0098150

Praise for

Phoebe

"Over the years veteran novelist Diane Noble has created a genre all her own. A word like *tender* might describe it best—touching, beautifully crafted stories filled with genuine sentiment and heartwarming truth. I had a lump in my throat the entire time I read *Phoebe,* and I reached for a tissue more than once. Only a writer of this caliber could introduce us to five main characters—Sarah, Faith, Ivy, Summer, and Stephen—in five different American eras, and have us truly care about all of them. Like a literary jigsaw puzzle, the various pieces of *Phoebe* fall perfectly into place until the timelines converge, creating one endearing portrait of the human heart."

—LIZ CURTIS HIGGS, best-selling author of *Thorn in My Heart*

"Skillfully winding three threads into a beautiful story braid, Diane Noble traces a promise of everlasting love through several families...and the God who proved Himself faithful to them all. A sweet treasure!"

—ANGELA HUNT, author of *The Shadow Women*

"In *Phoebe,* Diane Noble creates a witness to transformation, healing, and new lives. Diane's fans will love this story told with tender glimpses that gently move the reader across time and back, capturing the essence of sacrifice and love through the journey of a wooden doll. *Phoebe* is a hopeful story whittled from the finest wood by a skilled and steady hand. Enjoy!"

—JANE KIRKPATRICK, author of *All Together in One Place* and *Every Fixed Star*

"I was enchanted by *Phoebe,* a delightful novella filled with warmth and truth. I loved my vicarious travels through the decades with that little doll, and the ending had me smiling, albeit with tears in my eyes, sorry to close the cover for the last time."

—ROBIN LEE HATCHER, award-winning author of *Firstborn* and *Speak to Me of Love*

"In *Phoebe,* Diane Noble beautifully illustrates the way God's loving-kindness and faithfulness endure throughout the generations. The result is a skillful weaving of several stories that intersect in surprising and touching ways."

—DEBORAH RANEY, author of *A Scarlet Cord* and *Beneath a Southern Sky*

PHOEBE

Books by Diane Noble

Novels

Heart of Glass
At Play in the Promised Land
The Blossom and the Nettle
When the Far Hills Bloom
The Veil
Tangled Vines
Distant Bells

Novellas

Come, My Little Angel
"A Place to Call Home" in *A Christmas Homecoming*
"Birds of a Feather" in *Unlikely Angels*

PHOEBE

A NOVELLA

DIANE NOBLE

WATERBROOK
PRESS

PHOEBE
PUBLISHED BY WATERBROOK PRESS
2375 Telstar Drive, Suite 160
Colorado Springs, Colorado 80920
A division of Random House, Inc.

ISBN 1-57856-401-8

Library of Congress Cataloging-in-Publication Data

Noble, Diane, 1945–
Phoebe / Diane Noble.— 1st ed.
p. cm.
ISBN 1-57856-401-8
1. Christian fiction, American. 2. Dolls—Fiction. I. Title.
PS3563.A3179765P47 2003
813'.54—dc21

2003007139

Printed in the United States of America
2003—First Edition

10 9 8 7 6 5 4 3 2 1

For my daughter Melinda…

for your love and prayers,
for the joy I discover in you daily,
just because you're you!
I love you!

Let the beloved of the LORD
rest secure in him…
and the one the LORD loves
rests between his shoulders.

—DEUTERONOMY 33:12, NIV

Northwest Arkansas
Spring 1857

"Papa, how much longer?" Six-year-old Sarah stood near her father, hovering over his lap as he whittled. He was sitting on a stump near their covered wagon, talking to her ma about the day's work of getting the kinfolk settled into their rigs.

Sarah let out an impatient sigh, trying not to let her bottom lip pooch. Her twin sister Meggie never let her lip pooch, but Sarah always forgot to hold hers in, especially when she didn't get her own way. "Why did you make Meggie's first?" She was certain Meg was her ma and pa's favorite. Her twin never got into trouble, whereas Sarah seemed always to be headed to a corner to settle herself down, as Ma called it, on the three-legged milk stool.

Her pa bowed his big head and gave her a gentlelike nod, looking into her eyes. "Because I wanted you to learn patience, Sarah, to learn that good things come to those who wait."

"Doesn't Meggie need to learn it too?"

He laughed. "I don't think our Meg has an impatient bone in her body."

Sarah looked down at her limbs and frowned. "My bones are impatient?"

With that, her father, the captain of the big wagon company that surrounded them, put his head back and laughed out loud. Sarah smiled. Her pa's laugh was better than a banjo playing "Oh! Susannah." She sighed and leaned her cheek against his shoulder, watching his big hands carve the block of wood into a doll just for her.

Her bones were definitely impatient.

CHAPTER ONE

Eden's Pass, California
1935

Faith Green stomped on the clutch and, with her right hand, shifted down to first gear as the Model A lurched to a stop in front of Secondhand Rose. From the driver's seat she waved at the proprietor, Anna Rose Hill, who waved back as she peered out from behind a bit of tattered lace curtain hanging at the window.

Anna Rose then returned to arranging the display on the table beneath the window: a child's toy spinning wheel and basket of yarn spindles, a brass bed warmer, a stack of flour-sack dishtowels, a blue-speckled coffeepot with matching cups, a chipped porcelain baby's bathtub, and a wooden soldier propped up in the corner against a freshly painted toy cannon.

It was the little soldier that caught Faith's attention. Its carved face peered out at the world beyond the window, its painted eyes wide and curious, its round cheeks cheery, its well-formed mouth tilting upward at the corners as if with secret merriment. Even from this distance Faith could see the doll had been well loved, so smooth were its sweet features. She wondered—

and what a fanciful thought it was!—whether a child's caresses had caused the wearing away. Perhaps a father had carved it for a very young boy who didn't know toy soldiers were meant for playing war, not for kissing.

Faith's heart caught with a pang of longing for the father she'd never known. For another instant her gaze rested on the doll, and her eyes filled with sudden tears. She swallowed hard and brushed them away with her fingertips. Since her husband Finian's death last year, she'd become entirely too sentimental. She still wept at the memory of Fin whistling "Dixie" as he planted corn by the light of a full moon, and she got teary-eyed at the memory of his big voice booming out "When the Roll Is Called Up Yonder" while he stood beside her in church.

Lately, with her own loss still fresh, she wept at others' losses—as she did now, thinking about that unknown child and the loved one who had fashioned the doll.

And she wept because she wanted to remember her father and couldn't. He had died the same day she was born.

Now finished with her display, Anna Rose waved again, bringing Faith's attention back to the task at hand. Faith smiled in return and smoothed her mussed gray bob. She enjoyed racing the open-topped Model A along the dirt road leading from the lease, where the old family home stood tall and proud. But she always arrived at her destination looking disheveled and bright-cheeked from the harsh sun and brisk wind.

Just six weeks after dear Finian's heart plumb wore out and

hers nearly broke with grief, she upped and bought herself this old girl—she stroked the dashboard fondly—and set about learning how to crank the starter and shift from one gear to the next with a minimum of fuss and frog-leap. With each crank of the handle she still whispered a prayer of thanksgiving for the nest egg that Finian, God rest his soul, had left her.

The girls had called her foolish to spend such a sum in times like these, but—and the thought always brought a smile—Fin was likely looking over heaven's banister, glad for her charitable heart and pleased as punch with her spunk. Besides, the girls, with hands clasping hats to keep them from flying off in the wind, now hooted and hollered in glee every Sunday as Faith putt-putted them along the dirt road to church.

Truth was, when Faith had seen the good that Anna Rose was doing for the poor, she decided to help. The shop owner washed, ironed, and starched discarded clothing; cleaned and polished old furniture; fixed broken toys; and scrubbed rusted pots until they gleamed; then resold the items all for pennies—or gave them outright—to families in need.

The best medicine for mending her own heartache, Faith figured, was helping those who couldn't help themselves. And when she discovered that a vehicle was needed for pickup and delivery to Secondhand Rose—well now, she set about making sure it happened. Soon the car was needed more than ever.

First, she had tea with the ladies from three sewing circles in Eden's Pass: one affiliated with the Baptist's Cottage Hospital, another from the Community Presbyterians, and yet another from the First Nazarenes. After explaining what was needed, Faith said she would take to Secondhand Rose every new quilt the sewing circles could spare and every flannel baby blanket not needed for other charities. She couldn't sew a straight line to save her soul, but just weeks after her lessons, she could drive better than any other person in town, young or old, man or woman.

Oh yes, Fin would have been pleased. Faith grinned, patted her hair again, then with a sigh, stepped from the Model A. She closed the door with a thud and bent over the rumble seat to lift a cardboard box into her arms. It was large and awkward, filled with three newly stitched housedresses, four aprons, six sets of knitted bonnets and booties, two bright patchwork quilts, and a dozen flannel baby blankets, four edged with crocheted lace. All three circles had worked for a month on these projects and, as of this morning, had already begun their next month's work.

Anna Rose held open the door and smiled in greeting as Faith struggled through with the awkward carton.

"The lovely things you deliver are always the first to go." Anna Rose reached out to take two corners at the opposite side of the box. "Especially the baby blankets." Together the two women set the box on a nearby table with a thud. "Most folks give discards. You've managed to get your friends to give the best of what they make." Then she laughed lightly. "Don't get me wrong. In such times, we need anything and everything that can be given—leftovers included."

The women struggled across the small shop and placed the box on the floor. Anna Rose knelt beside the carton and held up a patchwork quilt to admire it.

"They're happy to do what they can." Faith smiled at the pleased look on Anna Rose's face. When Anna Rose had finished examining the new wares, Faith started for the door, then hesitated and turned back. "When I drove up just now, I noticed something in your window. It struck me as curious."

Anna Rose straightened with a laugh, still holding a tiny pair of pink booties. "Nearly everything I get in is curious in some way or another."

Faith frowned. "It's a doll. A toy soldier, it appears. Tucked back in the corner."

"I'll get it." Anna Rose placed the booties on a counter and headed to the window.

"Really, there's no need to disturb your display."

Anna Rose's laughter rang through the small shop. "Display?" She chuckled again. "I'll take that as a compliment. But really, the table is just another place to store the items that come in—at least until I can clean them up." She reached for the doll. "Such as this soldier boy. I just haven't had time to work on him."

Faith took the doll in her hands, turned it over, then tipped it back again so she could look in its face. "It *is* handmade," she said quietly. "I thought so." She turned it again, enjoying the solid feel of the heavy wood in her hands. Though immovable, the arms were well formed, fingers realistic and slightly curved, the legs straight and stout.

"Likely whittled by a father for his young son."

Faith nodded, again thinking of her own father. She touched the doll's worn face. The wood had smoothed with age and felt almost warm to her touch. "Curious," she murmured. "Even when I first spotted this doll in the window, a memory seemed to flit through my mind...but it's so elusive." She stared again into the toy soldier's face and touched its nose, its ears, its curly hair, with her fingertips. Looking up, she laughed lightly. "Then of course, it's likely my mind playing tricks. Since Fin passed..." Her eyes filled again, and she was unable to finish.

Anna Rose touched her hand. "You don't need to explain. I understand."

Faith handed the doll back to Anna Rose. "It may be a soldier, but it's beautiful. Do you know its history?"

Anna Rose touched the doll's cheek, tracing her fingers over the features. "I don't, dear. But I can tell you this: When I inspected it, I found a mark looking very much like a bullet crease." She shook her head as if in awe. "If I didn't know better, I'd say this toy soldier's been to war." She carefully gathered the small jacket into one hand, exposing the smooth wood of the doll's chest. "There, you see, the bullet sliced right across." She looked back to Faith. "And, though faded, you can see it's in a Union uniform."

"I wonder why a man, young or old, would take a wooden soldier into battle?"

Anna Rose shrugged. "That I wouldn't know." She walked back to the window and stood the wooden soldier by the toy cannon. "Though many who went off to war were little more than boys themselves." She shook her head as she walked back to Faith. "If only this doll could talk."

Faith chuckled. "Along with walls in old houses. Oh, the stories such things might tell." She started for the door, then turned. "I'll be back tomorrow with a sunbonnet quilt from the Community Presbyterians. I haven't seen it, but I hear it's a beauty."

Anna Rose trailed behind her. "They do such nice work."

Fingers resting on the brass door handle, Faith cast another glance at the doll. "You never did say who brought in the little soldier."

"It was that young Doc McKenzie."

"I haven't seen Doc since Ivy Magill's funeral. I hear he's leaving these parts."

"He and his new wife are heading to the Brazilian jungle to be medical missionaries."

"The wooden soldier must have been a childhood toy. He must have needed the money to give it up…though it couldn't have brought much."

Anna Rose nodded. "It seems to hold great value in his heart, though he didn't say why. I gave him all I could spare for the doll, but mostly to help him and his new bride." She paused. "And told him I would save it for him until he gets back from the mission field." Her eyes glistened as she glanced back at the doll. "Wouldn't dare sell it now."

"I'll talk to the ladies of the circles about what they might do to help Doc and his wife. I'm talking to the quilters' guild tomorrow about Secondhand Rose. I'll mention Doc's journey and see what they might do." She grinned. "Then there're the girls. They're always ready to help when presented with a need."

Anna Rose looked grateful. "These are hard times. But God's blessings have never been more abundant."

The bell above the door tinkled as Faith stepped back to the sidewalk in front of Secondhand Rose, musing about Anna Rose's compassionate heart. Everyone knew the widow often gave up food from her own table, had offered more than one coat or sweater of her own to comfort others. And there was that mark out back, in full view of the railroad tracks, letting hobos know they could find a hot meal at Secondhand Rose.

Anna Rose's limbs were too thin, as if she went without food so others had more. Yet her face was always bright with happiness; it was obvious she took greater joy in giving than receiving. That was what blessed her, blessed others, and this minute filled and warmed Faith.

She watched as Anna Rose moved to the rear of the shop. Before turning from the window, Faith let her gaze rest again on the doll. It would stand beside the shiny red cannon until Doc returned, reminding all who entered Secondhand Rose to pray for the young missionary and his bride.

And along with her prayers, Faith would continue to wonder about the faded memory so close to her heart that it made her weep, so elusive it seemed to edge her mind with light even if she could not say why it touched her so.

Crossing the Prairie
Spring 1857

I WILL LOVE YOU 4-EVER

"But what about Meggie's dolly? What will be on hers?" Sarah hugged her own doll close, then turned it over to examine the new-cut marks. She traced them with one finger. "What do the words say again, Papa?"

Her father chuckled as he sat down on an old stool from the back of the wagon and picked up Meggie's doll. Over near the cookfire, Law Mitchell played the harmonica, his music mixing with the sounds of singing and laughter and children's whoops and hollers. Farther way, cattle lowed, horses whinnied, and a smithy shoed to a *ping–pang* beat. "One question at a time, Sweet Pea."

Sarah loved it when Pa called her Sweet Pea. He never called anyone but her that. Sometimes he called Meggie Rosebud, but Sarah thought Sweet Pea was a much better name. She stuck up her chin and smiled at her papa. "What're you gonna write on Meggie's dolly's back?"

"The same thing we put on yours if she wants me to." He smiled at Meg and raised a brow.

Meggie shook her head. "I want mine different. I want a rosebud," she said, "'cause that's what I'm going to name my dolly. Rosebud."

Sarah thought about her sister's choice while her pa set about whittling a rosebud. Her lower lip pooched out before she could stop it, and tears filled her eyes.

After a minute, her pa looked up with a worried frown. "Child, what's the matter?"

"I can't even remember the words you put on my dolly," she said, moving closer to him. "I wish I had you write Sweet Pea on Phoebe."

Setting Meggie's doll aside, he reached for Sarah. "Your doll already has a name...and what we picked for Phoebe is just right." She sighed and cuddled against his shirt. It smelled of horses and cookfire smoke.

"It is?"

One arm held her snug as he took Phoebe from her. Then holding Sarah's hand with his big, rough one, he helped her trace the words. "I will...love you...forever," he read. Then she looked up from the doll straight into her papa's eyes to see him smiling down at her. "It's from a Bible verse," he said. "Found in the book of Jeremiah. Chapter thirty-one, verse three. Later I'll show you exactly where."

Sarah nodded and remembered. Slowly, she said the words her papa had taught her. "I have...loved thee...with an...ever...lasting love."

Pa smiled, his face looking like the sun had just come up. "That's what God says about you, Sweet Pea: 'I have loved thee with an everlasting love. Therefore, with lovingkindness have I drawn thee.' Don't ever forget."

She cuddled close to his big chest and whispered the words again so she would never forget. "I will love you forever," she said.

CHAPTER TWO

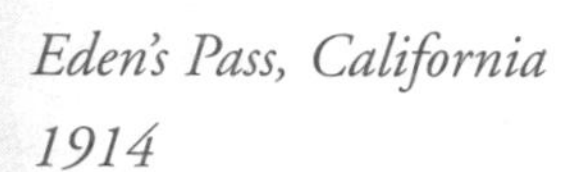

Eden's Pass, California
1914

If it hadn't been for the rustle of oleander branches and the tap of footsteps on the wooden porch, Ivy Magill never would have pulled back the dark drapes. And if it hadn't been for the worrisome sight just outside her door, she would have kept the brass lock turned and bolted, just as always.

But when she spotted a bundle the size of an infant wrapped in a blanket, she pushed the door open a few inches and peered out.

The air filled her senses with a heady bouquet of new-mown hay, fresh blooming jasmine, and sun-baked soil. She drank it in, savoring its cool, sweet taste. Since her loved ones' passing, Ivy had kept the big house shuttered and dark, the drapes pulled tight in every room—especially in the nursery at the top of the stairs. When Robby was alive, Ivy allowed the sunshine to stream through the nursery window in great bars of golden light. She would draw up the sashes, allowing the soft breeze to flow in, circle around her, and caress her with happiness as she held her little son in her arms.

Now she couldn't bear to open the nursery door. There, among the stacks of tiny shirts and nappies, Ivy would surely crumple to the floor never to rise again. She would remember the warmth of the child in her arms, the fresh-bathed scent of his dark curls. She would feel the clutch of his tiny fist wrapped around her finger. She would hear his soft breath and see the rise and fall of his chest as he slept.

And there, beside the empty cradle, she would weep until every tear had been squeezed from her, leaving only the dry bones of her soul.

If Dixon had lived, at least she would have someone to share her sorrow. But she was alone, her sadness so acute, her loss so overwhelming, she couldn't even pray for comfort.

Ivy stared down at the bundle at her feet and stooped beside it, her lips set in a grim line. She touched the blanket, tentatively. It didn't move.

Sorrow jolted up her spine, and she shuddered, remembering another fair June day, another still body wrapped in a soft blanket. For a moment, the memory took her breath away. Then frowning, she set her jaw and gathered the rigid bundle into her arms. Gingerly, she unwrapped the dirty blanket and gazed down in wonder at the wooden face that stared back at her. She touched its cheek, smoothed with wear, and almost smiled at its feel beneath her fingertips.

A boy whispered from behind the oleander: "You tetched, like they say?"

She narrowed her eyes at the tangle of branches and leaves, indeed feeling a bit tetched to be talking to a tree. "Who is *they?*"

A stick of a boy, about eight years old, stepped from behind the oleander. His reddish hair pointed up in peaks above a face that was more freckled than not. "Ever-body."

"*Every*body," she corrected.

He gave her a dour shrug before hopping down the stairs leading from her porch steps. "Tetched is what they say, all right." He stooped to pick up a fist-sized stone, then glanced purposefully at a pane in the parlor window.

"So it's you," Ivy said, meeting his defiant look with a steely gaze of her own. "If you're the one, I have a bone to pick with you, young man."

"Warn't me," he mumbled while letting his arm swing as if readying to let go of the rock. All the while he kept his eyes on her window.

"Wasn't," she said, "it *wasn't* me." When he didn't respond, she asked, "Is this your doll?" Then she softened her voice. "And I take it you've brought it as restitution for your sins?"

The sneer disappeared from the boy's face. "What's res-tui-tion?"

"Restitution. And it means payment. You've been throwing rocks at my house. You've broken three windows. So you brought the doll as payment for the damage."

The sneer reappeared. "I didn't break any ol' windows, and I didn't bring that ol' soldierin' toy as res-tui-ti-tion."

"Restitution."

"I didn't bring it for that."

"Then why..." Ivy looked down at the dirty wooden face, then back into the child's eyes. "Whatever would possess you to drop this thing at my doorstep."

"It was a lark," he finally admitted. "That's all." He dropped the stone and turned to leave. "I wanted to see if you'd come out, that's all."

When he reached the end of the sidewalk, she sang out, "That's far enough, young man. We haven't finished talking about what you owe me." The child glanced up in surprise as she continued. "If this doll isn't a gift—if you indeed left it here as a lark—then you still owe me restitution."

He paled beneath the freckles. "I told you it warn't—*wasn't* me. Besides, hit's a toy soldier. Hit ain't no doll."

"Isn't," she said.

The boy cocked his head, and something dark flickered in his eyes. He kicked at a crack in the sidewalk. "Isn't," he muttered with a sigh. "It isn't a doll."

Ivy closed the distance between them, then stooped so she could look directly into his eyes. "If you did throw the stones, you must work to pay for the broken windows. The one upstairs was thrown by someone with a very strong arm." She looked him up and down and nodded knowingly. "You look big enough to have done it. Certainly strong enough."

He studied her face. A proud smile played at the corner of his mouth. It occurred to her that he wanted to own up to being that strong but thought it might be better to dodge his way out of trouble.

"I guess I done it," he said finally. "I guess it was me." His thin shoulders drooped, and he didn't look so prideful now.

She gentled her voice when she spoke again. "I'll have a list of chores for you tomorrow. And I'll need to speak to your ma about it."

His eyes grew wide. "Oh no, that wouldn't do atall."

"But it must be done. I can't have you working about the place without your ma's knowledge."

"I-I'll tell her, then," he said. "I'll own up before I come back." The two bright spots that bloomed beneath the freckles on his cheeks told her that owning up was something he'd try to get out of.

She hesitated, then decided to give him the chance to tell what he'd done. "All right then, you go to your ma. Tell her what you've done. Ask her to drop by for a spell, and I'll speak to her about your restitution."

"She's awful busy. With the little uns and all."

Ivy figured that to be true. Many an afternoon, when she felt brave enough to peer through the windows, she saw the child's mother, a baby on her hip, several youngsters playing around her—some on their wide front porch, others in the yard. And each time she heard their laughter and singing and even their squeals, great waves of sorrow hit her afresh for little Robby and for Dixon, her dear husband. For the knowledge that there would never be such a family for Ivy Magill. For the bitterness deep in her heart.

"Nonetheless, I need to talk to her," she said to the boy.

The boy swallowed hard. "Yes, ma'am." Chin low, he shuffled down the walk to the dusty street. He glanced back shyly, swiped at his nose with the back of one hand, and then headed across the road. A wide overalls strap had slipped from one of his skinny shoulders, and the defeat in his face brought a sting to the back of Ivy's throat.

"I'll expect you at ten sharp," she called across the street to him.

The child didn't turn or even acknowledge that he'd heard her. She wondered if he would return. She doubted that he would tell his ma what he'd been up to, and Ivy was too soul-weary to cross the street and confront the child's mother. She sensed the boy knew that about her.

Promptly at ten o'clock the next morning a small knock sounded at the door. Ivy smiled as she set her cup and saucer of tea on the kitchen table and headed to the entry hall.

The boy looked up at her, his expression glum.

"You came back," she said gently.

He shrugged. "You said I had to."

"That I did. And I've made a list of chores."

"For the restitution." His pronunciation was perfect, as if he had been practicing.

"Yes, for the restitution," she said, smiling. "Please, come in." As he followed her to the kitchen, she asked over her shoulder, "You did tell your mother about this?"

When he didn't answer, she turned. "You did, didn't you?"

The boy swallowed hard and let his gaze drift to the kitchen window. "I thought it over and decided that 'stead of working I'd make a present of the toy soldier. I ain't got no use for it anyhow now that I'm growed up." He raised his chin. "That way, I don't have to tell Ma what I done."

"Remember what I said yesterday. Leaving the doll here as a lark doesn't count. You still need to tell your ma. Besides, she might not like you giving away your toys."

"Did you look at it?"

She raised a brow and nodded. "Only long enough to see that the little soldier's seen better days." Ivy poured buttermilk from a pitcher and set it on the table, tilting her head to show that the glass of foaming liquid was for him. He looked grateful and slid onto the chair, scooting it closer to the table. "And I wondered at the uniform it's wearing," Ivy said as he gulped down the milk. "It's awfully tattered and torn—like it's been nearly loved to death."

When he looked up with a white mustache on his lip, she smiled, resisting the urge to wipe it off. Before she could hand him a napkin, he swiped the back of his hand across his mouth. "It's from when I was real little," he said.

And he'd loved it once, Ivy reckoned. Loved it a lot. "I don't know your name," she said, her voice softer.

"Nate," he said, and then took another swallow of milk. He looked at her evenly. "What's yours?"

"It's Ivy Magill."

"Miz Ivy," he said with a nod, showing no matter how busy his mother was, at least she'd taught him manners.

The doll lay on the table where Ivy had left it last night, and she reached for it while Nate finished his milk. "To make restitution for something you've done wrong, what you give in return should be valuable. At least it should be valuable to you."

She pulled back the filthy rag cover and looked down into the wooden face. One blue eye looked helplessly out at the world; the other seemed to have been rubbed off completely. One cheek was polished and pink, the other mottled and rough. The finely formed lips were nearly lost beneath a thick coat of grime.

"I found it in a hatbox a long time ago," Nate said, leaning closer as if to have a better look. "Was my ma's. Then Miz Lucy made it a set of soldierin' clothes just for me, and so now it's mine." He shrugged one skinny shoulder again, blinked a few times, swallowed hard, and looked away. "Miz Lucy, well, she's passed on anyhow."

"Sounds like you miss her."

The boy shrugged again and leaned back against the chair rails, staring at the little soldier. "She gave the thing to my ma way back before I was borned. Said her brother brought the doll home from the war when she was a tyke. She made it a whole new set of duds just for me." He cocked his head at Ivy. "They're plumb wored out now."

"Worn," she said. "Plumb worn out."

He studied the doll's face, his expression pensive. "You can have it if'n you want." He shrugged as he traced one carved ear with his fingertip. "And I s'pose you're thinkin' it's not valuable." He set his chin at a stubborn angle. "But it is, Miz Ivy. It is."

Her voice gruffer than she intended, she said, "I thank you kindly then for it. I will accept it. I can see the doll means something to you, and restitution must involve sacrifice." Besides, now she wouldn't have to deal with meeting Nate's mother about the broken windows or the child doing chores. Ivy hadn't talked with the neighbors since Dixon and their baby passed of the influenza, and she didn't feel up to it now. She had drawn her dark drapes and refused to open the door when they called. She only wanted to be left alone in her sorrow. At first they were persistent, then gradually they stopped trying.

"Then I don't need to do nothin' else for the"—he hesitated—"the restitution."

She picked up the doll as the boy stood and scooted his chair under the table. "This is it. You're free to go—if you promise to never throw rocks at my house or anyone else's ever again."

His eyes met hers, and he nodded. "I promise." Then with a last glance toward the little soldier doll, he started for the door. "What are you going to do with it?"

She pictured the nursery, pictured the wooden soldier, cleaned up and natty, propped beside Robby's cradle in the nursery. She could pretend she was restoring if for her own little boy. Perhaps as long as she imagined it, her heart wouldn't ache. "I'll think of something," she said, reaching for the door handle to let Nate out. "I'll think of something."

As soon as the door closed, she headed upstairs and into the sewing room at the end of the long hall. She opened a window just enough to let in a crack of dim light. She laid the doll on her worktable. The tattered remnants of a Union soldier's trousers, blouse, faded red sash, jacket, and overcoat clung to its body. Even a small infantry cap had been tucked under the toy soldier's right arm. Carefully, Ivy removed each piece, folding it and laying it aside, down to the drawers and socks and leather boots.

She opened the window a few more inches and then marveled at the even stitching on the uniform, the attention to detail—as if the maker was determined to show this toy had been in the war. She traced her finger along the spiral-shaped hollow that cut across the toy soldier's chest as if a bullet had grazed him.

She suspected Nate's Miss Lucy had given it this dramatic touch for the boy's sake.

Moving the doll into the light, she turned it this way and that, examining the wood, the whittling marks, the age cracks, the grime gathered through what surely had been decades of love. Wondering how it would clean up, she rummaged in the back of a cupboard for a pot of linseed oil.

Eagerly she dipped the corner of a soft rag in the oil and scrubbed the doll's right arm, attacking the sticky coat of grime. When the downstairs clock struck noon, she had only cleared a small streak from the elbow to the hand. Frowning, she kept scrubbing, this time upward toward the head. As the layers of dirt receded, the whittle marks began to show.

By three o'clock Ivy had cleaned the face, and to her amazement both eyes were in place, likely as colorful as the day they were painted. They looked up at her, shiny and bright, pink cheeks round and gleaming, one with a dimple, perfect little lips curved in a smile.

Ivy smiled with delight. The doll seemed to be coming to life. Her fingers couldn't move fast enough as she scrubbed and polished one hand, then the other. Dip and scrub. Polish and shine. Again and again she repeated the proccss until her fingers ached. It was almost dusk when a knock sounded at the front door. It had been so long since anyone visited, it took Ivy a moment to recognize the sound. She hurried down the stairs, still holding the doll.

She opened the door. Nate stood in front of her, looking down at his shoes.

"Why, son," she said, her heart dropping. She wondered if he had come back for the little soldier. She was becoming attached to it. How could she let it go?

"I came to 'pologize," he said quietly, still looking at the ground.

She couldn't help the sigh of relief that escaped her lips. "You did?"

He nodded. "My ma—well, seems she found out what I did."

Ivy's heart caught again with new worry. "You mean that you gave me the doll?"

"Nah. She said I could do what I wanted about that. It was about throwing the rocks. My little brother told on me. Ma said she'd tan my hide if I didn't hightail it over here and say I'm sorry." He glanced down the road to where his mother stood with a baby on one hip. She gave him a stern nod of encouragement.

"Are you? Sorry, I mean?" Ivy said, looking back to the boy.

He ventured a glance up into her eyes. Ivy could see he'd been crying. "Yes, ma'am. I shouldn't of done what I did. And that ain't all. She says it don't matter one iota about the doll. Givin' it to you, I mean. She says I still got to work off what I done."

Ivy again looked to Nate's mother, looking stern and forlorn at the edge of the road. Ivy waved and smiled, letting her know she would take care of the boy.

"I have an idea," she said to Nate.

" 'Bout my workin' for you?"

"Yes sir," she said with a smile. "I'm cleaning up your toy soldier, and you can help me."

His face brightened. "You are?"

She laughed lightly, surprising herself at the sound. "Would you like to come in and see what I'm doing with it?"

His expression brightened. "Yes ma'am."

"I just found out your toy soldier has blue eyes."

"I already knowed that," he said. "Miz Lucy painted them on. Said they matched my eyes. But I didn't know they still showed." He trotted behind her to the staircase, and they started up. "But, well, you see, Miz Lucy, blue eyes or not, she said the doll had a history and that it was fittin' to have soldierin' clothes."

Ivy paused at the landing, looking down into the child's upturned face. "Do you know anything about that history?"

He shrugged. "Nah. Just that it was special to Miz Lucy."

"No," she said, "is better to say than *nah.*" She continued up the stairs, the boy trailing a few steps behind her.

"Miz Ivy," he said when they reached the top, "you know what you do that's jes' the same?"

"Just the same as what?"

"As Miz Lucy." He grinned up at her. "You're always atellin' me not to say *warn't* or *ain't* or *nah.* Just the same as she did."

He stopped at the top of the stairs, and a few steps ahead of him, Ivy turned and waited for him to go on. "Miz Lucy was my godmother, though I called her Nanny till I growed up enough to call her Miz Lucy."

"Grew up." Ivy took his hand, unable to stop smiling. "Until you grew up enough."

The boy tucked his hand in hers as they continued down the hall to the sewing room.

Oregon–California Trail
Spring 1857

"Mama, this is the prettiest I ever saw," Sarah said in awe. Her mother drew her needle through the bright red calico. "Will it have lace?"

Ellie Farrington shook her head as she wound the thread around her finger, tied a knot, then held up the dress for Sarah's approval. "We don't have any, sweetheart. Maybe when we get to California, we'll find some there."

Sarah's lip threatened to pooch, but she caught it just in time and gave her mama a shaky smile instead. "But Phoebe wants lace," she said softly. "Oodles of it. She told me."

Her mama scrunched her eyes the way she always did when she was thinking of something funny. But Sarah didn't think Phoebe's wanting a tad of lace was funny at all. "Why does Phoebe want such fuss?" her mama asked.

Sarah thought about it for a minute. "Because she wants to be a lady."

With a smile, her mama drew her close. Then she reached for Phoebe and helped Sarah pull the dress into place, fasten the back buttons, and tie the sash into a bow at the waist.

"Ooh," Sarah breathed, holding Phoebe out at arm's length. "She's beauty-full."

"It takes more than lace to make a lady," her mama said after a minute.

Holding Phoebe close to her heart, Sarah considered her mama. She was round and lovable, soft in just the right places for hugging. Her hands were strong and brown, and her legs never seemed to get tired, even when she walked alongside the wagon all morning. Best of all, Sarah liked how her eyes seemed to dance when she was thinking pleasant thoughts, like when she rubbed her back and stretched because of the baby she carried in her tummy. *What a wonder!* Mama would say to Pa, and her eyes would look prettier than ever.

Her mama was the best lady in the whole wide world. And she didn't wear a bit of lace. "Maybe Phoebe doesn't need any lace," Sarah said, now snuggling on Mama's lap. "Even in California."

Her mama's head rested atop Sarah's. "How do you know?" she asked.

"'Cause Phoebe told me."

CHAPTER THREE

Ivy Magill gave Nate a pot of linseed oil and a rag and showed him how to clean the years of grime off the doll. "Rub along the grain," she said, "the same way you would sand a fine piece of furniture."

Intent on his work, the boy bent over the soldier doll, dipping and scrubbing, then holding it out to admire. Ivy sat across the table, smoothing the tattered, dirty uniform and thinking about the new clothes she would make using the old one as a pattern.

"I have it in mind," she said, "to dress this doll just the same as your Miss Lucy did, perhaps in nice felt trousers and a bright blue jacket, some fine leather boots."

Nate wrinkled his nose in delight. "Just the same?" He scrubbed the wood for a time, then looked up again. "What're you gonna do with it then?"

She pictured the nursery, the empty cradle. "I'll put it with my keepsakes. They're in a very special place."

He leaned forward. "Can I see 'em?"

Something cold filled her heart, nearly causing her to shudder. No one else had gone into Robby's nursery since he died. "No," she said and turned toward the window before his look of disappointment could make her cry. "No. It's a place only I can go."

As the boy scrubbed with linseed oil, Ivy kept her gaze on the thin strip of window. This project that had fallen into her hands was more than simply fixing up an old soiled doll. Her need for the doll's transformation ran deep. "Think how distinguished your soldier will look," she said, turning back to him, "once he is cleaned up and handsome again." She hesitated, the boy's expression tugging at her heart.

"You said *your* soldier," he said, "but it ain't mine no more."

"Isn't," she corrected but without as much enthusiasm as before. "Anymore." She paused, searching his face. "You'll soon see," she said after a moment, "this little soldier will be as good as new. Since you know what the original uniform was like, you can help me decide exactly how to make the new one." She gave him what she hoped was an encouraging look.

Nate stared at the rag in his hand, and Ivy wondered if it was because he was considering where to rub next, though she somehow knew it was something deeper. Robby's sweet image came to her mind, pushing aside the freckled face of the child in front of her.

For a moment the room was silent except for the wiping of the linseed cloth.

"What's this?" He pointed to a place on the doll's back. "What's it say?"

Ivy leaned toward the doll, touched the lettering and shook

her head. "I can't make it out. It looks like the letter *I,* maybe the word *will.*" She frowned. And perhaps the word *love.* Yes, I believe that's it. Something about love." She looked up at him. "Can you make it out...the letters *L-O-V...?* Maybe the *E* was rubbed off years ago?"

"I never saw it before," he said without enthusiasm. "But I don't see things right anyway. I don't see any ol' letters."

She glanced at him sharply. "What do you mean?"

He shrugged. "Don't matter anyhow." He stood, dropped his rag, and walked slowly to the door, his shoulders so drooped that one strap of his overalls slipped off. He shrugged it back into place and tromped down the stairs.

Thinking she couldn't bear to see his sadness, Ivy didn't follow. Instead she busied herself over the Singer machine, the rhythm of her feet on the treadle keeping time as imagined childhood scenes of Robby marched into her heart.

She pictured the joy Robby would have taken in the little soldier. Her son would be nearly four years old now, just the age for playing with such toys. She could almost see him sitting cross-legged in the nursery, trotting the doll across the floor, making battle sounds in his throat—the *Pow! Pow!* of cannons, the blast of guns—just as all little boys loved to do. Galloping on an imaginary horse, listening to his daddy tell of the war and the great Mr. Lincoln.

Ivy worked into the night. By the time the big hall clock struck three, she had finished the doll's trousers and double-breasted jacket. By dawn she had fashioned a pair of miniature leather boots for its feet.

She stitched a small red neck scarf, pricking her finger twice. Now and then memories drifted into her mind. The sounds of Robby's voice as he formed his first words played like a tender melody in Ivy's heart. "Ma-ma," he babbled, holding out his arms for Ivy to lift him up. And "Da," he said with a giggle, reaching for Dixon, who stood grinning in the doorway. "Da!" their son chortled.

They embraced that day, Dixon holding Robby in one arm and circling the other around her. A perfect circle. One she thought would be everlasting.

Everlasting? She almost choked on the word. Once a sampler made by her grandmother had hung in the dining room. A bright sunrise graced the top, a colorful sunset at the bottom. And in the center were the cross-stitched words,

FOR THE LORD IS GOOD;
HIS MERCY IS EVERLASTING;
AND HIS TRUTH ENDURETH TO ALL GENERATIONS.
PSALM 100:5

She dropped her head, and her tears began. What kind of merciful Lord would take those she loved from her arms? *What kind of mercy is this? What kind of love?*

"Oh, Father," she whispered, "help me. I don't think I can go on. The heartache...the bitterness... I can't get rid of them. They're like weeds in a garden, so tangled and thick they're choking out everything good that might grow in my heart." Holding her head in her hands, she continued to weep.

Just past sunup, Ivy was descending the stairs, holding a damp cloth over her swollen eyes, when a knock at the front door broke into the gloom of her heart.

She moved slowly to the door but brightened when she saw Nate looking up at her with a smile.

"Good morning," he said politely. But he stood on one foot then the other, glancing past her to the stairway.

Laughing at his renewed enthusiasm, Ivy stepped back to let him in. Without another word the boy raced up the stairs to the sewing room.

For a moment, he just stared at the doll, now lying in the middle of the worktable, its new clothes in place. "Looks the same," he said in awe, "only better'n before. You done even better than Miz Lucy done."

"Miss Lucy did."

"Miz Lucy *did*," he said with a sigh and smiled up at her again. "I had an idea last night."

Ivy picked up the doll to examine her stitching. "And what might your idea be?"

"I kind of, well, miss the soldierin' doll, and I thought, well, maybe, I might could make another one." The hope suffusing his face nearly broke Ivy's heart.

"Whittling's a lot of hard work, and you must have the right tools." She spoke gently, thinking about the impossibility of the child making a toy soldier that would resemble the one he obviously still loved.

He nodded. "You said yourself that I got strong arms. I was thinking maybe we could find a block of wood, maybe ask Mister Krebbs to loan us some tools, and I could start whittlin'. I could start even today whilst you're sewing."

He leaned forward. "There's an old woodpile down by the general store—out back where it looks like no one cares about it." He hesitated, not taking his bright-eyed gaze from her face. "We could go together," he suggested, then sat back, waiting for her answer. "Mister Krebbs mightn't pay no mind to me by myself."

Ivy could count on one hand the times she'd been outside her house since the day they buried Robby in the churchyard. Mortimer Krebbs at the general store delivered a box of cornmeal, flour, vegetables, and fruits in season, with two bottles of buttermilk every Tuesday, leaving them on the back porch where he would find his payment under the mat and a list for the coming week. She ventured to the bank every first of July and withdrew enough from the savings account Dixon had opened before his death to last until the same day the following year.

But this? Walking down Main Street in broad daylight, hand in hand with a child who'd been throwing rocks at her windows. Her heart skipped at the thought. Tetched? She gave him a shaky smile. Well, indeed, she just might be.

"That sounds like a fine plan," she said, peering through the crack in the sewing room window. "And it looks like a fine day to make such a journey."

Nate grabbed her hand and pulled her to the stairway. "Let's go!"

She patted her hair. "Well now, child. I must put on a hat and gloves. I dare not be seen in public looking such a fright."

Nate stood back and looked her up and down. "My ma don't even own a hat, and I think she looks right pretty. So do you, Miz Ivy."

She was surprised by the quick tears that pinched that place behind her nose. "Well now," she said again, blinking rapidly, "I do think I'll need a hat as protection from the sun." She smoothed her skirt with her hands. "But other than that, I suppose I'm ready."

She opened the cloak closet, pulled out a straw hat, and placed it on her head. She adjusted the brim and straightened the ribbon tails. Then she peered into the small mirror beside the front door. Her eyes were still puffy, but other than that, she supposed she was presentable.

The sun hung round and warm in the summer sky when Ivy and Nate stepped outside her front door. With a sigh, she drank in the beauty of the blue sky and breathed in the scents of late spring, the wafting fragrance of distant orange blossoms.

"Altogether lovely," she whispered, lifting her face to the sun. At her side, the boy tilted his face into the warmth of the sun and sighed noisily. The sound made her smile. In fact, it seemed the boy was always causing her heart to lighten of late. She reached for his hand, and they started down the dusty street.

A horseless carriage rattled by, and a man in a derby blew an ooga horn and waved merrily. Ivy coughed in the dust it left behind, but couldn't help smiling. "My goodness, what I've been missing," she said to Nate with another small laugh.

A few minutes later another contraption sailed by, a bicycle with a front wheel as tall as Nate, a smaller one in the back, a jingling bell on the handlebar. The cheerful traveler pedaled vigorously and tipped his straw boater as he passed.

"Have you ever whittled or carved anything before?" Ivy asked when they'd gone a quarter mile or so.

"Nah. My pa, he's too busy to show me." He sighed again and then looked up hopefully. "Besides, Ma says a body's gotta have the patience of Job to teach me anything."

"It takes patience to work with any child," Ivy said.

The boy fell quiet for a few steps. "It's different with me." He looked out at a stand of orange trees. "My teacher, Miss Parrott...well, she just gives up trying. Sits me in a corner most of the day."

"Could it be she does that because you've misbehaved?" Ivy thought of the rocks, the windows, and thc countless other shenanigans the boy had likely pulled. "Maybe that's why."

"Maybe," he said. "But I see things backwards. Can't help it. No matter how hard I try. Miss Parrott thinks I'm funnin' her when I write words backwards."

"Are you? Poking fun at your teacher, I mean?"

He lifted one skinny shoulder, then let it droop. "Sometimes, I reckon," he owned. "Ever-body—*every*body laughs, so sometimes I pretend I'm doin' it on purpose." He looked up at her as if expecting her to get after him for doing such a thing.

But Ivy gazed down in the child's face. "Maybe you can show me," she said. "Before I met my husband I was a schoolmarm. Maybe I can help."

A slow whistle escaped his lips. "You were?"

She nodded. "A long time ago."

"What happened to Mister Magill?"

At the top of an oak tree a scrub jay scolded, and the *sizzlezings* of grasshoppers flying across their path punctuated Ivy and Nate's soft footfalls. "He died," she finally said. "Three years ago."

The boy didn't answer right away. "It hurts your heart somethin' fierce to lose somebody you love."

She remembered why the boy knew such a thing. He'd lost Miss Lucy. Ivy had been dwelling on her own loss, not considering his. It shamed her.

"Miz Lucy told me one time that in such times God comes closer to us than we can ever imagine, because he knows what it's like to lose somebody you love."

Ivy stopped and looked down at him. "Miss Lucy told you this?"

His eyes were round and sad. "I think she knew she was gonna die and wanted me to know." They walked on in silence for a few minutes. "She said God knows what it hurts like because it was his own Son that died a terrible death. It broke his heart so much that the whole earth turned dark when it happened." He stopped and looked up at Ivy. "That's how come God can comfort us."

This child knew of God's love, accepted his comfort without question, yet Ivy had chosen a different road, one in which she had wrapped herself in lonely sorrow. She swallowed hard. "Your Lucy was a wise woman."

"Yes ma'am."

They walked up a slow rise in the road, and the general store came into view. A wagon rumbled by, drawn by a swaybacked mule, and they stepped to the side of the road to let it pass.

"Miz Lucy, she made me larn—*learn* something from the Holy Bible before she passed on. Made me say it over and over till it was hidden in my heart. That's what she called it—a golden nugget that needed to be hidden right here." He thumped his chest.

They crossed the road in front of the general store. "What was it she taught you?" She stepped up the wooden stairs, Nate trailing behind.

When he reached the top stair he took a deep breath as if preparing for a recitation, then began: "It's the twenty-third Psalm. It goes like this, though I might not get it right. Sometimes I get the words mixed up."

"That's all right," she said gently. "Why don't you try?"

He halted and looked at the sky, knitting his brow and biting his bottom lip in concentration. "The LORD is my shepherd," he said slowly; "I shall not want." His voice was low and reverent as he continued through the whole chapter, each word pronounced correctly, even the *thee*s and *thou*s, just as Miss Lucy had taught him.

"Yea, though I walk through the valley of the shadow of death," he said, meeting Ivy's gaze with sad eyes, "I will fear no evil: for thou art with me; thy rod and thy staff they comfort me."

He swallowed hard, then continued. She thought he might cry, but instead his little freckled face lit up when he came to the last verse. "Surely goodness and mercy shall follow me all the days of my life," he said dramatically, "and I will dwell in the house of the LORD for ever!" He hopped down the stair then back again. "That one is my favorite," he added, still smiling. "'Cause it means that Miz Lucy, she's dwelling in heaven with God, and someday I'll be there too."

Before Ivy could comment, he rushed on. "Miz Lucy made me say it over and over, told me never to forget that God was with me, that he was feeling ever bit of hurt that was in my heart."

"Does it help? I mean, when you're sad?"

"I still cry sometimes. At night when ever-body else is asleep. Then I remember Miz Lucy and how she told me that my heavenly Father would be with me, would wrap his arms around me and pull me on his lap just like I was his little kid. And he would hold me tight."

She tried to swallow the sting in her throat. "Let's see about that block of wood, shall we?"

Nate marched to the counter and asked about the wood in back. But before Mortimer Krebbs answered, he looked up in surprise to see Ivy standing behind the boy. "Well now, Miz Magill. It's good to see you out and about."

Ivy stepped closer to the counter and gave him a brisk nod. Talking with the boy was one thing, getting into conversation with others of the townsfolk was quite another. "We're here about the woodpile out back. Would you mind if we look for a suitable piece for carving?"

"Why, no. Not at all."

"And whittlin' tools?" Nate asked at her elbow. "Do you have any we might borrow? It's just for a short spell."

Mortimer Krebbs rubbed the top of his bald head. "Well now, I'll have to check my tool supply. But I imagine I'll find something." He rummaged around in a small wooden box of rusted implements behind the counter. After a moment he held up four chisels of varying sizes, two tapered metal punches, and a small saw. "Ah yes. Here we are. Will these do?"

Nate's eyes were shining. "Yes sir, I believe they will."

All looked too large for the child's hands, and most were covered with layers of rust. "Is there a charge?" she inquired.

"Not a cent," Mr. Krebbs said. "And you can keep them. I've no use for any of these."

"Thank you," she said, then looked pointedly at Nate, who murmured his own thanks.

It didn't take long to find a solid block of oak in the woodpile, and the two started for home. The boy chattered amiably, his obvious excitement about the whittling occupying his mind.

But when they reached Ivy's house and set about trying to figure where to start carving the wood, they looked at each other in dismay.

"Maybe we need a pattern," Ivy said. She reached for the toy soldier and placed it in front of the child. Next she found a sheet of drawing paper, and put it before him with a fat pencil. "Why don't you try drawing the head first, then the body and arms and legs?"

He nodded and bent over his work, holding the pencil in a white-knuckled grasp. He bit his lip in concentration and began to draw.

He attempted everything backward, painstakingly drawing fingertips first, then moving the pencil to where the doll's shoulder ought to be, then attempted the same thing from foot to torso. The lines wobbled off into space, hopelessly lost, like unwound twine. After a few minutes, Nate threw down the pencil. "See," he said defiantly. "I told you so. I can't do it!" He ran from the room and tromped down the stairs.

But before he reached the front door, Ivy caught up with him. "Child," she said, putting a gentle hand on his shoulder, "don't you go stomping off like you're giving up." She fixed him with a stern look. "Don't tell me you're a quitter."

He sniffled, and when he looked up, his chin quivered. But it jutted out, which was a good sign. "I ain't a quitter."

"I'm *not* a quitter," she said, reaching for his hand.

Oregon–California Trail
Late Spring 1857

"There's a crossing coming up, child." Pa halted the big Appaloosa, and Sarah leaned against him, enjoying the feel of sitting high on the horse with her pa's arms holding her tight. The big river lay off in the distance, looking like a silver snake. "I want you to promise you'll sit quiet-like while your ma drives you and your sister across."

Sarah nodded solemnly. "Can I help Ma? You said Meggie and me had to help her lots these days."

Her father chuckled. "Not this time, Sweet Pea, but I want you to watch closely. Someday you can drive the team yourself—just like your ma."

Sarah played with the tip of her long braid, thinking about such a deed. "I want to be just like her," she said.

"I can think of no better ambition," her pa said. "You watch closely and do exactly as your mama says."

"I will," she promised. "But sometimes Meggie doesn't mind so good."

He raised a bushy eyebrow, warning her not to tattle. "It will be like sitting in a rocking chair," he said. "And you'll need to hold on tighter than you've ever held on before."

"I will," Sarah said, "and so will Phoebe." She looked into the face of her beloved doll, then covered her curly head with kisses.

When she looked up, her pa was squinting at the river again as if he was imagining the wagons going across. Sarah felt a twinge of alarm at the worry around her pa's eyes. She put her hand in his. "It will be all right, Papa," she said. "You'll see."

CHAPTER FOUR

Ivy placed her hand on Nate's. "Relax," she said, "and let your hand follow mine."

But the child's knuckles remained white, and his fist rock hard, the stubby pencil sticking up like a flagpole.

"Here, try this," she said quietly and again tried to move his hand. It wouldn't budge.

"I-I can't," he grumbled, his tone now more belligerent than sorrowful. His mouth turned down at the corners. "Just like I told you, I see ever-thing wrong. I can't do it." He threw off her hand and stood. "I told you so." The scowl deepened. He tossed a glance at the toy soldier. "It's just like always," he muttered. When he lifted his eyes to hers, his face showed mingled dismay, anger, and sorrow. "It don't matter nohow."

Ivy didn't bother to correct him. She felt helpless, wanting to reach out to him, but not knowing how. His hurts were too deep, his frustrations obviously too great for a few minutes spent in Ivy's workroom to make a difference.

"Maybe it just doesn't matter," she whispered to herself, her thoughts going to Robby and Dixon. For a brief time, she'd thought God might have sent the child to ease her loneliness, but now, meeting his defiant expression, knowing the hurdles the boy had ahead, she didn't think she had the energy to give him what he needed. It didn't matter who sent him or why. With a heavy sigh, she turned away from the boy.

Minutes the later the downstairs door slammed, then Nate's padding footfall disappeared into the sounds of the summer morning.

All day, Ivy mulled about the boy and his heartache. Just before sunset, she ventured out on the front porch to sit in the swing, something she hadn't done in years. Sounds of laughter and squeals and song spilled from the open windows of Nate's house across the street. Now and again, a child or two or three would run from the house, skip rope, play ring around the rosie or tag, then hop up the stairs and head back inside. Only to run back out, perhaps with another child or two in tow. As the sky grew darker, Ivy realized that she hadn't seen Nate. Not once.

Finally, Nate's mother called to the children that it was time for bed. After a few whines and complaints, reluctantly, the little ones marched back up the stairs and into the house.

Still Ivy sat on the porch swing, watching the moonrise. Beside the house, crickets creaked and sawed, and in the distance frogs kicked up a song that nearly drowned out the crickets.

Across the street, the children were likely in bed. Every window but one was dark. And in that window where a lamp's golden light still glowed, silhouetted behind a pull-down shade, Nate's father pulled his mother into his arms. Ivy could almost hear the tired woman's sigh as she laid her head on her husband's shoulder.

Ivy turned away and swallowed the sting in her throat, willing herself not to cry from her heart's longing for Dixon. "Oh, Lord," she whispered, "why is my darkness near impossible to overcome? I cry to you again and again..." She stared into the ink-black sky. "But you allow my suffering to continue. I can't be rid of it. I can't."

The child's words came back to her, almost as if upon the breeze that ruffled the leaves of the big eucalyptus next to the porch: *I still cry sometimes. At night when ever-body else is asleep. Then I remember Miz Lucy and how she told me that my heavenly Father would be with me, would wrap his arms around me and pull me on his lap just like I was his little kid. And he would hold me tight.*

She couldn't bear to think about Nate, there in his room, crying for his nanny, crying from the disappointment of his day with Ivy. She stared at the big house until the last light was extinguished. The loneliness of the darkening night made her shiver. But as she climbed the stairs to her bedroom, the image brought into her heart by the child's words burned strangely bright.

She made her way down the hall, lit only by dusty moonlight, then hesitated at the nursery door. For a moment she rested her hand on the small glass knob, wondering if she had the courage to enter the room. It was important. Something...*Someone*...inside her heart told her it was. She pushed open the door.

Crossing the room, she first lit the lamp that sat atop the small child's chest of drawers, then dropped to her knees beside the empty cradle.

Picturing Jesus on the day he blessed the children, she thought about her baby. What if he had been one of them on that day? She remembered the warmth of his little body in her arms, and she imagined handing him to her Lord.

A peace settled into her heart as she pictured it.

"Father," she wept, "why couldn't I have seen this earlier? Why couldn't I have known?"

And Dixon, her precious husband...if he had been standing beside her on that day by the Sea of Galilee, he would have carried their son to Jesus himself. Gladly. Joyfully. Triumphantly.

She laid her arm across the side of the cradle and lowered her forehead to rest in the crook of her elbow.

"My child is yours," she said quietly. "You lent him to me for a season, and now it's your arms he's resting in, not mine."

For the longest time she knelt, as a new brightness dispelled the dark in every corner of her heart.

When she looked up, the first thing she saw was the toy soldier standing beside the lamp. She rose slowly and moved toward it. She picked up the doll and examined it.

Three faint lines of carved letters on the doll's back had intrigued her when she rubbed off the thick grime. Now, curious to see it again, she unfastened the small felt jacket and traced the lettering with her fingertips.

I WI
LOV Y
4 EV R

"I will love you forever," she whispered in wonder, surprised she hadn't managed to fill in the words before. Tears filled her eyes, creating a watery veil as she looked across the empty room. Only now it didn't seem so empty. It seemed filled with love.

I will love you forever. Just as she would hold her beloved child and husband in her heart during all her days on earth, so would her heavenly Father hold them in his arms, the two of them, and Ivy, when she joined them someday. A complete circle. A love with no beginning, with no end.

I will love you forever.

She held the doll close to her heart, cherishing it for the message it had brought. Then releasing it, she looked down into its round-cheeked face.

The doll wasn't hers to keep. How well she knew that now! She propped it against the lamp and surveyed the room as an idea came to her from someplace deep inside.

First thing, she would pull back the curtains so plenty of sunlight could flood the room. She would set up a little desk near the largest window. And set a lamp in each corner for the darkest of wintry days.

She almost danced around the room, picturing how she would arrange it. Plans flew into her mind nearly too fast to retain.

Bookshelves, she would need at least three. And oodles of books, simple ones with brightly colored pictures. Also, those that would serve as read-aloud books, *Tom Sawyer* and *Huckleberry Finn* to start with. And a chalkboard on a stand for the front of the room. And a smaller hand-held slate. And boxes and boxes of chalk sticks.

She would see Mortimer Krebbs about ordering the supplies she needed. But walking to the general store wouldn't be the first thing on her agenda. She smiled as she turned down the lamp. No, there was a far more important stop to make first.

The following morning, just past sunup, Ivy stepped onto her porch and fixed her gaze on the big house across the street. Already, above the birdsong, sounds of laughter, singing, and shouting spilled from the Victorian.

Nate was standing in the front yard, but when he saw Ivy, he turned away from her, the slump of his skinny shoulders speaking louder than anything he might have said. Unwilling to be deterred—by the child's diffidence or her own staccato heartbeat—Ivy put her chin in the air and crossed the street.

By the time she had climbed the porch stairs to the front door, the boy had disappeared around the side of the house.

Before Ivy could knock, the door was thrown open by a little girl with two missing front teeth. "Hallo," the girl said, grinning. Her tongue played with the spot where her teeth should have been.

"I-I'm here…well, that is…" Ivy took a deep breath, feeling lightheaded. Her earlier euphoric courage was fading fast. "Your mother," she managed to murmur, "is she at home?"

"Ma!" The little girl yelled without turning around. "There'th thomebody here to thee you!"

A pale, curly-haired woman appeared a moment later, at first looking puzzled. When she recognized Ivy, a smile lit her thin, tired face. "Miz Magill," she said. "What a surprise!" She moved beside her daughter and gestured toward the interior of the house. "Please, please come in!"

A pleasant glow warmed Ivy's heart as she stepped inside. She had followed only a few steps when Nate's mother turned and laughed, catching her hands to her cheeks. "Oh, Miz Magill, please forgive me. We've never been properly introduced. I'm Summer—Nate's mother, as you likely know."

"I never knew your name, but it's because of Nate that I've come." Ivy followed Summer who was now picking her way across the threadbare rug littered with building blocks and wooden train cars. "Please call me Ivy," she said to Summer's back.

Summer stopped almost midstep and turned—pleased, by the look of her—and took Ivy's hand in both of hers. "Well, thank you, Ivy. I've wanted to get acquainted ever since we've been neighbors."

"You have?"

Her pale cheeks flushed. "Truth is, I've just been so busy…" She looked embarrassed and picked up a handful of alphabet blocks from a horsehair chair, dropping them on the floor. "And then the others—the Joneses from up the road and Mister Krebbs, too—told me that after your tragedy, you didn't want callers." Her smile softened. "But there's no excuse for more recent times. I should've been over for a visit long ago." She pointed to a chair near the parlor window. "Please, sit down. Marci Jo needs tending. I'd better get her."

A few minutes later, Summer was back with a child of about two years. Her hair was the same sunshine color as her mother's, and as she whimpered sleepily, she watched Ivy with big, round, watery eyes. Ivy smiled at Marci Jo, who smiled right back, then settled against her mother and popped her thumb into her mouth.

"You said you're here because of my son," Summer prompted, a tired sadness behind her eyes.

"Yes. I'm afraid I've deeply offended him."

Summer tilted her head with a frown. "I can't believe you've done any such thing." She shifted Marci Jo to a more comfortable position. "Nate is a handful. I figured you sent him home for good reason yesterday." She shook her head. "Though he wouldn't tell me why. I had planned to head your way this afternoon—find out if he'd done something I needed to know about." Her face looked wearier than ever.

"Send him home for good reason?" Ivy was astonished. "Oh, goodness no! He left on his own accord. He was trying his hand at drawing a design to whittle into a piece of wood. He found the task difficult."

Summer's expression gentled. "He has trouble with such things. He gets impatient with himself. Tries too hard, then just gives up." Marci Jo, eyes heavy with sleep, leaned her head against the crook of her mother's arm and sighed deeply.

"Nate helped me clean up the doll he brought over," Ivy said. "We scrubbed and polished our fingers nearly to the bone. And then I made new clothes. A brand new little uniform, just like it had before."

"Nate told me," Summer said. "He said you did some fine work, better than Miss Lucy's."

Ivy didn't want to admit it, even to herself, but she told Summer her thoughts. "I know now that Nate wasn't ready to let it go. It was something very special to him—because of Miss Lucy. I was too distracted by my own reasons to see how he needed to have that little soldier back. Then your son came up with the idea to whittle a new toy soldier."

"But he couldn't make sense of how to do it?" Summer's eyes were full of understanding.

Ivy nodded. "He had such grand plans."

"His mind is quick. He sees things he wants to do, but when he sets about doing them, they come out jumbled. Backwards."

"It would be a difficult task for anyone to carve a doll. I should have realized how frustrating it would be for an eight-year-old."

Summer held up a hand and spoke quietly so she wouldn't wake the sleeping child on her lap. "Don't blame yourself. Nate is a special boy. He needs special attention, attention it seems no one has time to give him." She looked embarrassed, and Ivy knew she must be blaming herself, in spite of the half-dozen children who took every minute of her time.

"Even his schoolteacher seems to have given up on him. Says he refuses to learn and that he causes trouble for the others at school." Summer shook her head. "He's falling further and further behind. The saddest thing is, just lately he acts like he doesn't care."

"But he does."

Summer shifted Marci Jo slightly. "I put him off without meaning to, but there's so much else to do. I try to keep Nate busy so he'll stay out of trouble, then he gets into it anyway. He's always been a tumble of energy and ideas. When he was just a little thing, he loved nothing more than to sit with me for hours, looking at picture books. Now he wants me to read to him... because he doesn't know how to read by himself." She swallowed hard. "Just like his nanny used to...read him books with words instead of pictures. He wants me to help him learn to read." She gazed down at Marci Jo, and when she continued, Ivy had to lean forward to hear her voice. "Trouble is, I just don't have time anymore." Her mouth held tight, she looked back to Ivy.

"Nate wants to read?" Ivy said gently. It was a start.

Summer nodded. "He's smarter than all the rest. But he just can't seem to make sense of reading and writing and ciphering."

"Maybe I can teach him," Ivy said. "I've been thinking about it. I used to be a schoolmarm, long before I married Mr. Magill. I've worked with children who see things backwards. I have some ideas about how he can learn. If Nate is willing to try, I'm willing to help him."

"Instead of attending the school in town?"

"Maybe we can work especially hard to help him catch up. If he'll work with me, he can eventually join his classmates—knowing how to read and write and cipher." In her excitement Ivy spoke even more earnestly than she had before. "I have nothing but time on my hands."

Summer frowned. "You would do that for him…for us?"

"Truly I would."

Summer's expression softened as her gaze rested on Marci Jo, sleeping peacefully in her arms. "I'll talk to him," she said. "But he can be stubborn. I can't promise that he'll be willing."

Ivy laughed softly. "Stubborn? I already figured that out. But then so am I."

"When do you want him to come for his first lesson?"

"I'm on my way to order supplies right now. But all we'll need to start is a table, a chair, and some books. I've got all those, so we'll begin this afternoon, if Nate is willing."

From somewhere in the back of the house, a child giggled, another one yelled, and the little girl with missing teeth lisped a nursery rhyme.

"I can't promise," Summer said, shifting the child in her arms and preparing to stand.

"May I help?" Ivy stood and reached for the toddler, and Summer handed her over with a sigh.

She rubbed her back. "I think another little one may be on the way." Her face glowed as if she was expecting her first child.

For a heartbeat, Ivy held Marci Jo close, breathing in the sweet, powdery scent of her skin. "One more thing," she said. "If you ever need a rest, just call on me. I would love to watch any of your little ones."

Summer slipped her arm around Ivy and drew her close. "How blessed I am that our Lord continues to add to our family."

Ivy expected Summer to rub her stomach, but instead, the younger woman's gaze met Ivy's. It wasn't the baby, but Ivy herself, Summer meant.

Ivy didn't stop smiling all the way to Mortimer Krebbs's general store.

All that afternoon Ivy waited for Nate to arrive for his first lesson. The big clock in the hall ticked and chimed hour after hour, and still the boy didn't knock on the front door. Ivy tried to keep her hopes up, but when night fell, she knew he wasn't coming. At least not today.

Nor did he come the following day.

On the third day, Mr. Krebbs delivered the large chalkboard, the wooden desk with inkwell and folding lid, a dozen boxes of chalk, a stack of brightly colored primers, writing paper and pencils, and a pen with a bottle of ink.

While Mr. Krebbs carried in the supplies, from the corner of her eye, Ivy spotted Nate slouched against a post on his front porch. She hoped curiosity would get the better of him. But he turned and headed back into the house, letting the door slam behind him.

That afternoon as Ivy carried the cradle to the attic and placed the stacks of Robby's tiny shirts and flannel blankets in the trunk next to the cradle, she planned the first day's lesson, praying the boy would gather his courage and knock on her door.

It wasn't until the middle of the night that it came to her. Ivy grinned and sat up in bed. *Of course!*

In the pale light of predawn, Ivy lit a lamp, headed up the rickety attic stairs, and rummaged in the trunk for one of Robby's blankets. For a moment she buried her face in its folds. Then, clutching it close to her heart, she climbed down the stairs and padded down the hallway to the schoolroom.

The soldier doll stood in its usual place atop Robby's dresser, its drawers newly stocked with chalk and pencils, paper, and bottles of ink.

"Ah, my little doll," she murmured, picking it up. "I don't know your history, but I think you've surely brought much love to other children, just as you once brought it to the lonely, troubled little boy across the street." She carefully wrapped it in

Robby's blanket. "It's time for you to bring some hope into this child's life once more." Holding the doll close to her heart, she started down the staircase to the front door.

The sky was pink in the east as she crossed the street, and the first rays of golden sunlight were just stretching across the sky as she laid the small bundle at Nate's front door.

Then she quickly crossed back to her house. She drew open the drapes in every room to let in the morning. She sat in the parlor rocker, resisting the urge to see which of the passel across the street would be the first to open the front door. She prayed it would be Nate.

Soon the sounds of children spilling into the summer day carried through her open windows. Laughter and song, just as she always heard.

Then the summer air fell quiet, strangely so. Murmurs of awe followed a heartbeat later.

Still, Ivy resisted peeking out. Hands folded on her lap, she prayed.

The padding of small footsteps could be heard on her walk, then on the stairs and across the big porch. Ivy thought she might weep before a small, shy tap sounded at the door.

She opened it. Nate stood before her, smiling up at her. "Good morning, Miz Ivy," he said. He held the soldier doll in his arms.

"Good morning," she said. "Are you ready for your first lesson?"

He swallowed hard. "Yes ma'am."

She stepped aside so he could enter. "I have a plan for our first day."

He trailed behind her as she climbed the stairs to the new schoolroom. "A little reading from *Tom Sawyer*—have you heard of him?" She looked back at him.

He shook his head.

"He was a boy who reminds me of you. Full of spunk, but bright as a new copper penny."

"Really?"

"Really."

His eyes grew big and round when he saw the nursery's transformation. He slid into the student desk with no prompting and stood the little soldier beside the inkwell. "You did this just for me?"

"Yes."

Ivy pulled out a sheet of lined paper and a thick-nibbed pen. "Now, let's begin," she said, placing the paper on the desk before him. "We'll start with your name."

"But why?" Nate persisted, taking the pen. "Why are you doin' it, I mean?"

"Someday I'll tell you," she said gently, thinking of the gift the child had given her. "But for now, I want you to write your name."

"But it'll be backwards."

"That's all right," she said, then added, "for now."

Nate dipped the nib into the inkwell, bent over the paper, and began to write laboriously from right to left.

"That's fine penmanship," Ivy said and patted him on the shoulder. "Fine indeed. I want you to come with me and see for yourself." A moment later she watched their reflections in a looking glass as she held up his paper.

A smile of wonder overtook his freckled face. "Nate McKenzie," he whispered in wonder. "I did it!"

Sarah's ma sat on the wagon bench, whip in hand, ready to pop it over the oxen team. She whispered so quietly that Sarah figured she must be praying—just as she always did before heading into danger. Then she nodded to Pa that she was ready. The twins sat directly behind her in the wagon, watching through the front opening of the hooped canvas cover.

The rig moved into the river, and Sarah yelped with delight.

"Shhhh," Meggie reminded her. "Pa said to be quiet."

But Sarah couldn't help herself. "Yahoo!" she called out, then clapped one hand over her mouth dramatically.

The wagon swayed, making flour sacks and grain barrels slide, but Sarah wasn't afraid, because her ma was driving the team. And her pa was out in the river on the big Appaloosa just in case he needed to help with the oxen.

She settled back to enjoy the rocking-chair ride and to listen to the calls of Joel and Law, the cattle hands helping with the fording. Then Law yelled, all excited-like, "You're gonna hit the sandbar, Miz Farrington! Pull to the side, pull to the side!"

"Current's too strong," Joel cried, sounding grieved to death. "You're gonna lose 'er."

Sarah stood up to see what the commotion was all about.

The wagon tipped, and Sarah tipped with it. Barrels, trunks, and pails shifted. A hatbox toppled, and a packet of her ma's letters, tied with a pretty ribbon, spilled out. Sarah reached to catch it, but Meggie hollered and grabbed hold of her sister's arm. They both slid to the side of the wagon with a *clunk*.

Sarah settled down on the seat with a huff, indignant that Meggie had to help keep her from falling out of the wagon. She brushed off her skirts, then glanced at her ma to see if she was about to get scolded. But Ma was still busy popping the whip over the oxen's backs.

Meggie's freckles looked dark against her pale skin. She reached for Sarah's hand and held it tight. Sarah grinned, pleased that she might be braver than her sister after all. She looked out at her pa and waved with her other hand. This was a fine ride, with the smell and the spray of the river, her ma driving the big wagon, and her pa watching from the sandbar.

A fine ride indeed.

CHAPTER FIVE

Monterey, California
1904

The setting sun hung just above the ocean as Summer McKenzie rode bareback along the beach. Summer tossed back her tangle of pale curls and halted the tall mare to watch as the waves turned from deep green to flame. It was her favorite time of day, her favorite place to catch the disappearing sun. The salty breeze touched her face, and she sighed, thankful she would never need to leave her home by the sea. She had been born here, all her kin lived nearby, and her husband Eli had promised to buy her an ivy-covered cottage near the ocean.

Behind her a familiar voice shouted, and her heart leaped at the sound.

"Summer!" Eli galloped toward her, waving his hat and grinning wider than she had ever seen him grin. Except maybe on their wedding day. When he reached her, he slid from his horse, then clasped her around the waist to help her to the ground.

"Dear Eli," she said, matching his smile with her own, "you

do appear to have come upon good news." She hoped it was about the cottage.

For a moment he didn't speak but simply gazed into her eyes. "You're beautiful," he finally said, his voice hoarse, "standing here all rosy-cheeked and windblown. I must be the most blessed man on this planet."

She giggled and ducked her head, feeling shy, but loving how he loved her. He reached for her hands and drew her close, resting his head atop hers. After a moment he circled his arm around her shoulders, and they walked along the wet sand, leaving the horses grazing in a patch of sea grass.

"You must have something pretty important to say." Summer looked up at Eli. His face reflected the glow of the setting sun, but there was something in his expression that made her stop quite suddenly. She searched his face as a troubling darkness settled into her soul. "You wouldn't be butterin' me up now, would you, Eli McKenzie? Butter me up with your sweet talk, then tell me somethin' I won't like?" Her voice was teasing, and she waited for him to laugh and tease her back.

"I do have something serious to tell you," he said quietly and raked his fingers through his copper hair, something he often did when he was nervous. "It's good news." He took her hand and led her to an outcropping of granite not yet touched by the incoming tide. Overhead the gulls cried, and farther out an otter lay on its back in the seaweed banging on an oyster shell with a small rock.

They sat down. "You sound happy, but your eyes look chary,"

she said, leaning her back against him. She heard him release an even deeper sigh.

"You know how I've wanted to get out on my own, get out from under your father's thumb."

She leaned forward and turned to look straight into his eyes, but he let his gaze drift from hers. Eli's working for her father had been a sore spot since he took Eli in before the wedding. "He's been good to us. Doesn't he pay you a decent salary?"

Eli nodded. "He does."

"And he owns the biggest cannery in town. You go to work for someone else, and you'll make half the salary." To Summer no discussion was needed. She couldn't understand why Eli constantly brought it up.

"Your father treats me like a child."

"He treats you like a son," she argued. "The son he never had," she added for good measure.

Eli reached for her hand and held it between the two of his. "I can't stand it much longer, sweetheart. He rides me constantly. Tells me all I'm doing wrong in front of the others." Eli sighed. "I don't mean to sound ungrateful, but I never meant working for your father to be a permanent thing." He shrugged. "There, I said it."

He'd said it before, but never with so much conviction.

"And there's something else," he said. "We can't go on living with your folks this way. We need a place of our own."

She brightened, again picturing the little ivy-covered cottage.

"Well now," she said carefully, "we'll have to just see about something else then, won't we? Something close by. Maybe on a sardine boat. They're always looking for extra hands." She laughed lightly. "Working in Daddy's factory won't last forever." She squeezed his hand. "I promise."

His gray eyes met hers. "It's not yours to promise, Summer. It's up to me to make a change—and do it before we have a family on the way. And I aim to do just that as soon as I can." He fell silent for a few minutes. Only the lonely cries of the seagulls carried on the wind over the restless mutter of the surf.

Fear chilled her heart. "You've found something else, haven't you?" she finally whispered. "That's what all this is about." She held her breath, awaiting his answer.

Eli nodded. "I'd hoped it would be good news for us, that you'd see it as a grand adventure, a chance to get ahead."

"Adventure." The word came out in a squeak. "That sounds like you're going someplace far away."

He grasped her hand tighter. "Not *I*, Summer. *We.*"

She flung his hand away from her and stood. "Going away? From here?"

He swallowed so hard his Adam's apple bobbled up and down.

"I— We can't do that!" Her voice had taken on a shrill edge, but right now she didn't care if she sounded like a fishwife. "I can't. I won't!" Before he could speak, she went on. "This is our home. My mother and father...my friends...*everyone* lives here. When you asked me to marry you, you never said we'd have to leave."

"Our life together is what counts."

She hated the quiet, reasonable sound of his voice, so she tossed her head, crossed her arms, and looked out to the now-dark sea. He stood and came alongside her, but when he moved to hold her, she turned abruptly away. "Where?" she whispered, her voice shaking.

"I answered an advertisement in the back of *Gentleman Farmer's Almanac—*" He paused, looking at her with a mix of sadness and hope in his eyes.

She bit her tongue and waited impatiently for him to finish.

"It's for selling farm equipment."

"You fancy yourself a traveling salesman." Her chin quivered. "Jokes are made about such men." Hot tears filled her eyes. "Surely you can't mean it." What would her friends say?

"Where?" she asked again, the word nearly lost in the sound of the surf. "Where would this traveling salesman need to travel?"

"I requested something in Salinas Valley, so's you could live near your kin, but—"

"But there wasn't anything?" She pressed her lips together to keep from weeping aloud.

"No, I'm sorry. The only available position is in the south. Near Los Angeles."

"Los Angeles? It's just a dusty town in the middle of nowhere."

"There's lots of ranching nearby. The company tells me the whole region is ripe for the picking."

Los Angeles? They might as well be heading to the moon. Dry. Flat. Dusty. Not much more than a pueblo. Filled with cowboys. Not at all a sophisticated city like San Francisco. Move there, lock, stock, and barrel? She couldn't let him do it. Not to himself. Not to her.

Drawing in a deep breath, she looked up at him and tried a shaky smile. "I-I'm sorry I fell apart," she said. "It's just such a shock."

A hint of relief crossed his face. "I knew it would be...a shock, I mean. But I'd hoped that we could set out with a sense of adventure. Together."

She placed her hand in his again, finally, and they turned back to the horses grazing a few yards down the beach.

"Promise me you'll think kindly about it," Eli said after a few minutes.

Oh yes, Summer would think about it. But not kindly. And only long enough to figure out how to talk Eli out of his hare-brained plan. For now she gave him a guileless smile. "I'll think about it," she said sweetly. "I promise."

He let out a boyish hoot and again tossed his hat in the air. Summer's eyes smarted with quick tears. She would not be a partner to his joy.

Summer was wrong. Eli refused to change his mind. As they waited for word about Eli's job, she pleaded day after day, but nothing convinced him of the error of his ways. Not her cajoling, not her tears, not even her huffy silence.

Finally came the news that Eli had landed a new job in the San Gabriel Valley, at a place called Eden's Pass, just an hour by train from Los Angeles. On the same day, Summer discovered she was pregnant. But when she told Eli about the baby, she hurried to add, "You go without me," she said. "If it's a traveling salesman you want to be, then go ahead. Travel."

The light in his eyes faded. "What about our baby?" His voice dropped, filled with sadness. "Now we have more than just the two of us to think about."

"I don't care. I want to be near Mother during my…my confinement."

He hesitated as if weighing her words, then his gray eyes turned steely. "I've let you go on and on long enough. It's time for me to put my foot down. You're coming with me."

"I'm not."

He stepped toward her. "We'll find a home to raise our children properly, on our own like grownups instead of your parents' children." Then he hesitated, searching her face. His voice softened. "Please, Summer. Let's try it for a year, maybe two. If you still feel the same way, I'll bring you home."

"And you'll stay here with me?"

He didn't answer. Where was the love they once shared? Why was he making her suffer so? Finally, she shrugged. "All right, I'll come along. I'll try it for a time." And during that time she would continue to show him how wrong he was. She would convince him that they both needed to return to her beautiful home by the sea.

Within the week they boarded a southbound train. They stopped first in Los Angeles, then headed out on a track appropriately called a spur. They passed through El Sereno, Alhambra, Pasadena, and Sierra Madre, and all looked surprisingly habitable. Friendly even, with houses of whitewashed adobe and red tile roofs. But by the time the train halted in Eden's Pass, the villages with real houses had disappeared. Spreading out in all directions, except north where the boring terrain was broken by mountains, were acres of brown, dismal, dusty flatlands. She saw no structures at all besides a row of shops that made up the main street.

"This is it?" She set her straw hat firmly on her head and frowned. "There must be a mistake."

She stepped onto the station platform and waited for Eli to see the stationmaster inside about mail from his new employer. An incoming locomotive let out a blast of steam, a clatter of pistons, a shriek of wheels, as it halted on the tracks nearest Summer. She waved the steam away from her face and coughed dramatically as Eli dragged their trunks toward where she stood.

"There was a letter waiting," he said once he reached her. "The company leased a house in our name. Belongs to the company, of course. But it's a place to call home."

"You asked them to make such a decision for us?" She made sure her anger showed on her face.

He flushed. "Apparently there aren't a whole lot of houses available."

She turned her gaze pointedly toward the barren landscape. "I understand," she finally said, her voice chill with bitterness.

"Soon there will be neighbors. More are moving here by the day," he said, trying to lift her spirits. "You'll have friends someday."

"Someday?"

After they stopped at the mercantile for supplies, an hour's wagon ride brought them to her new home. It lived up to Summer's expectations, set in the midst of weed-covered brown hills, and though Eli told her it was only hours from the ocean by wagon, one-half hour from the mountains, she wouldn't have known either were close by.

"Too much gray haze," Summer said glumly when she saw the weather-beaten old house, rising crooked and forlorn on a dusty hill. She rubbed her back, reminding him of her condition. "And I don't suppose you'll be around long enough to fix it up," she complained a few minutes later as she walked through the off-kilter doorway. "I've already figured you'll be on the road most of the time."

The only answer she received was the slope of Eli's shoulder lifted in a tired shrug. *Why won't the man talk to me anymore?* She glared at him. Maybe she wouldn't speak to him the rest of the day just to show him her misery. Didn't he realize the sacrifice she'd made, leaving her family and the only home she'd known?

She rubbed her back again, thinking that she ought to have a better life than this. She deserved it. But Eli didn't seem to notice. He turned away just as he always did and set about scrubbing down the kitchen and fixing the crooked door. Exhausted, Summer retired to the dirty horsehair sofa the previous tenants had left in the parlor.

Eli left six weeks later. She found his note on the rickety kitchen table.

Dear Summer,

You see no good in me, and it grieves me to say this, but maybe you would be better off without me. I thought my love for you might be enough to heal your bitterness. But your bitterness seems only to grow stronger with each day that passes. I will see to your needs and the baby's, but I need to stay away for a while and decide what is best for us both. I figure you want to go back home to your folks. I will send you there, just as I promised. I have decided to take a second job in town to earn enough for your train fare. I will send money once a week through the post office by the train station. You will need to fetch it yourself, perhaps with the help of a neighbor down the road.

Your husband,
Eli McKenzie

With a deep sigh of self-pity, she folded her arms on the table and, bending over them, wept bitter tears. Why had the man brought her here only to abandon her?

The tears flowed daily. Four days after Eli left, she was lying on the sofa, still sniffling, when a knock sounded at the front door. She rose and headed to answer it, figuring it was Eli, come to his senses at last. In the short distance from the parlor to the door, she practiced the bitter tirade that would flow from her lips.

But when she yanked open the door, a dark-haired, middle-aged woman stood in front of her, holding a pie with two big, bright yellow potholders. The fragrance of peaches and cinnamon filled Summer's nostrils.

"Dear one," the woman said softly, "I've come to welcome you to the neighborhood." Her gaze seemed to take in everything at once, from Summer's red eyes to the disheveled room and back to Summer, looking surely as miserable as she felt. There was no judgment or pity in the woman's expression. Only compassion.

Summer's lower lip quivered. "You brought this for me?" She couldn't look up from the pie.

The woman nodded. "Yes, child. I did." She smiled. "May I come in? I'll slice a piece for you." Summer moved aside, and the woman bustled past her without hesitation and headed to the kitchen. "Are your plates in here?" she called over her shoulder.

Too late, Summer realized she hadn't washed the dishes since Eli left. With a heavy sigh, she padded along the bare floor to make up an excuse for the mess. But when she arrived in the kitchen, the woman was already pumping water into the sink atop the dishes.

"I could heat some water," Summer said, wearily starting for the kettle on the stove.

"Won't hurt to wash up in cold water just this once." The woman helped herself to the bar of Fels-Naptha, swishing it in the water until bubbles piled high.

"I-I'm sorry... Things are such a mess..." Summer's voice faltered. "It's just that—well..." Sobs shook her shoulders, and she buried her face in her hands. "I just can't seem to get around...to it...not since...Eli..." She hiccuped and sobbed some more. "Not since he...left me."

The woman frowned. "Oh dear, I knew there was a reason I needed to come tonight." She wrapped her arm around Summer's shoulders and steered her back to the parlor. "There, there, I want you to put your feet up and stay put. I'll do around in the kitchen a bit, then come back with that pie."

Summer nodded mutely.

After a few creaks of the hand pump, the splash of water, and some clatters of plates being washed, the woman returned with a tray set for two. The plates held wedges of pie, and to one side sat two cups of steaming tea.

Summer's mouth watered, and she closed her eyes as she savored her first bite. "I haven't asked your name," she said after a moment.

"Lucy," the woman said, sitting on the opposite end of the horsehair sofa. "Lucy Elliot." She smiled gently. "Newly widowed."

"My name is Summer McKenzie," Summer said, and her voice turned sour as she added, "Newly alone too…" Her eyes filled, and setting the pie plate aside, she had another good cry. "M-my husband's left," she said when she could speak again. "Left a few days ago…"

"I'm so sorry, dear," Lucy said softly. "Is there anything I can do for you?"

"I-I'm expecting a baby. And now I'm all alone," she said, weeping harder. "I don't know what to do."

Lucy sat calmly, compassionately, beside her. "Your house is the farthest out from town," she said after a few minutes. "I know how lonely it can be. My husband brought me here from Temecula years ago. It took me awhile to grow to love the peacefulness of the open land." She touched Summer's hand. "I'm a ways down the road, but I can stop by and check on you…if you like, that is."

Summer ignored the offer, dwelling instead on her wretched state. "How can I do this?" she whispered, feeling dazed and weak.

"How can I do this alone—take care of...well, everything...all by myself in this ugly monster of a house?" Her fingertips rested over the place where the baby grew as her voice turned bitter. "How dare Eli do this to me? To us?"

She glanced around the old house. "He said he was going to find me a little ivy-covered cottage, just like we always planned. Now he's gone, likely off to greener pastures. Now I have no cottage. No husband." Her laugh sounded more like a bitter snort, even to her. Then a new torrent of angry tears overtook her, and she sobbed and hiccuped until there surely were no more tears to cry. She didn't notice Lucy had left until her weeping stopped, and she looked up to blow her nose.

She crawled off to bed, awash in misery, imagining what she would say when Eli came crawling back. Hanging onto the satisfaction of such a day, she finally fell into a troubled sleep.

Ma halted the oxen at the far side of the river, and Sarah scrambled from the wagon, Meggie following at her heels. Pa galloped the Appaloosa toward them, a grin a mile wide on his face.

"Did you see us, Papa?" Sarah called. "Did you see how Ma drove the wagon?"

"That I did," he said, his eyes shining with pride. He nodded to their ma. "That was some fancy driving, Miz Farrington."

Their ma looked pleased. "Girls," she said, "get in the shade of the wagon now. The sun's too hot."

Sarah clambered back inside, eager to pretend she was driving the wagon, just like her ma had done. She would shout "Yee-haw!" at the team, and off they would rumble, Sarah sitting tall on the bench, Meggie, Rosebud, Phoebe, and all. Giggling to herself at such a plan, she scanned the wagon bed, then looked behind the flour barrel and sacks of grain, even in her bedding. "Where's Phoebe?" she called out to Meggie. "Where'd you put her?"

"I didn't put her anywhere," Meggie said.

"Where is she then?" A knot was already forming in Sarah's insides. She climbed from the back of the wagon and peered underneath, but Phoebe was nowhere to be found.

Meggie jumped down beside Sarah and shot her a worried frown. "You were holding her in the wagon," she said, "while we were crossing the river."

Sarah's chin trembled, and her voice was only a whisper. "When we went sliding across." Then she gulped a deep breath and let out a wail, bringing her mama and papa on the run.

"Child, whatever is the matter?" Papa said as he swept her up in his arms.

"I want Phoebe," Sarah sobbed. "I want Phoebe!" And she buried her head against her papa's shoulder. He held her tight, but even that didn't help.

"I must get back to the crossing," he said after a minute. "I'll help you look for Phoebe later. When all the wagons have crossed, then we'll go downriver and take a look."

She wiped her eyes with her fists. "All right, Papa," she said, sniffling. But all she could think about was Phoebe being scared and alone as she floated down the river. "I will love you forever," she whispered.

CHAPTER SIX

The following morning another rap at the front door roused Summer from her troubled sleep. She splashed water on her face from the pitcher at the washstand, ran a comb through her tangled hair, pulled her wrinkled dressing gown closed, and padded barefoot to the door. Hope vanished that the early morning visitor might be Eli when she peered through the adjacent window and saw Lucy waiting.

"Lucy," she said when she opened the door, then added pointedly, "you're up bright and early." Instantly, she was ashamed for guarding her sleep so selfishly. "Come in, Lucy. I'm glad you've come." She moved aside so Lucy could enter. Then she noticed a small wood-slatted wagon behind Lucy. Clearly she had pulled it here from her house.

Lucy saw Summer's quizzical look and smiled. "Some supplies to see you through for a few days." Summer stood staring, astonished at the bounty, as Lucy handed her a small pail of brown eggs. "Take these first, child. And be mighty careful. I carried them all the way here. I don't think I broke a one."

Within minutes, the two women working together had unloaded bundles of dark grainy bread and buttermilk biscuits, a sack of fresh-picked tomatoes, another of sweet purple onions, and a pail of thick creamy milk and carried everything to the kitchen.

"There now," Lucy said, brushing off her hands, when they had finished, "that should keep you for a while." She started for the door.

"Please," Summer said, trailing after her, "must you leave so soon?" The house would be too quiet when she left. Lucy's smile and her soft laughter were almost contagious. Summer didn't want to see them go.

Lucy turned, her hand resting on the door handle. She brushed a stray lock of hair from her forehead. "I thought you might want to be alone."

"I recognize I'm not good company," Summer said with a sniff.

"I've never been a body to sit around and think about my circumstances too much," Lucy said, though not unkindly. "If I stay, I'll not give you any pity…or listen to it from you. Only serves to bring my spirits down, and I'll not have it."

Summer stepped backward, stunned. "Well now, I certainly am not one prone to such behav—" She stopped, knowing she didn't speak the truth. "It's just that…well, things couldn't be worse. With Eli leaving and all. And there's been no one to talk to…only myself. I suppose I need a friend, but one who is willing to walk with me through my valleys." She held up her head, her heart full of self-righteousness.

She waited for Lucy to tell her she would be that friend. Instead, Lucy studied her as if waiting for something else, but

Summer couldn't for the life of her figure out what. She shrugged. "My life is full of sorrow right now, and if you don't want to listen to me, to help me, then that's up to you." Her eyes filled, and she sniffed again.

Lucy merely nodded, but when she reached the door, she paused and looked again to Summer. "I'll be back in a few days to see how you're doing. I think you'll have plenty of food till then." She paused. "If you need anything, I'm not far down the road. Look for the small brick house with dark green trim."

Summer swallowed the sting in her throat, surprised that her attempt to control Lucy's actions hadn't worked. She bit her lip to keep from pouring out more bitterness. "As you wish," she said, lifting her chin.

Lucy smiled and gave her a friendly nod as if she hadn't noticed. She turned the doorknob and stepped outside. Through the doorway, Summer noticed that behind Lucy the brown hills seemed to have a golden glow in the light of the morning sun. A covey of quail chatted and chirped and fluttered as they scratched the ground, and a squawk of scrub jays filled the air.

Summer sat down on her porch steps with a great *humph* and watched Lucy set off along the dusty road. She longed to call after her, inviting her to come back and enjoy the morning together.

The days passed slowly as Summer awaited Lucy's return. She stewed and fretted and blamed everything she saw moving—from a scraggly old hen that annoyed her in the front yard to the jackrabbits that stared in her windows—for her misery. Eli had left her. After only two years of marriage, he had left. So much for his vow to love and cherish her forever.

Every day, she padded barefoot around the lease, sometimes pulling up turnips or beets, other times pulling rotten peaches from the tree and throwing them at jackrabbits, pretending each perplexed little face was Eli's.

Finally on the fifth day, Lucy returned. This time she was in a wagon drawn by a swaybacked mule. Seeing Summer on the porch, she waved merrily as she approached.

Summer narrowed her eyes, bent on showing her displeasure that Lucy had taken so long to return. She stood slowly and rubbed her back as a reminder to Lucy of her delicate condition.

Lucy didn't seem to notice. "I've come with supplies!" she called out, swinging from the wagon bench. She walked toward the house with a spry swing, her face lit in a warm smile of friendship.

"Thank you," Summer said without emotion. She pursed her lips into a wrinkled-prune expression and sniffed.

Lucy stopped at the top step to look Summer up and down. "My, my. I do believe this valley sunshine agrees with you. Your skin's turning golden, and you've got some pink in your cheeks. And you're not looking so peaked and thin."

Summer didn't respond, not caring that Lucy saw her sulking.

"Besides the food, I've brought you something special today," Lucy said, gesturing back to the wagon. "You want to help me unload?"

Summer sauntered behind Lucy to the road, rubbing her back each step of the way. "You've been to town?"

"Yes, as a matter of fact, I have." Lucy handed a sack of string beans to the younger woman. She bent over the wagon to retrieve another sack, this one filled with fragrant, ripe tomatoes. Then she reached for still another, filled with apricots.

But Summer wasn't paying much attention to the fruit and vegetables. "You've got something special?" Her heart caught. "A letter must have come in then, money from Eli. That's the special thing you mentioned?" If she hadn't been holding two sacks, she would have clapped her hands together. "Now I can go home!"

Lucy turned, her expression sad. "No, child. It's not. I did stop by the post office, but nothing has come in for you."

Summer turned away, her thoughts toward Eli turning stormy once more. She shrugged and muttered, "I thought it was too much to ask for."

Lucy touched Summer's arm. "It's not too much to ask for, child. Not at all."

"But it didn't come."

"Maybe there's a reason."

"If Eli's not coming back, I want to go home to Monterey."

Lucy gently turned Summer toward the house. "Let's go in and put these things away, then we'll talk."

Without being asked, Summer lit a fire in the rusty stove, pumped water into the kettle, and put it on to boil. She pulled out the tin of tea and two cups. She fought to keep her voice pleasant when she turned to Lucy and asked, "Will you stay?"

Lucy smiled. "Why, yes. I would be delighted."

Minutes later Summer sat down beside Lucy on the front porch, looking out at the pumping wells. "Thank you for all you're doing for me. I'll repay you once Eli sends me some money."

"There's no need to repay me, Summer. I know you're in need, and God has been good to give me an abundance of riches. I feel blessed to share them with you."

She should have known Lucy was wealthy. Summer was likely no more than a charity case to her. Tears of self-pity stung her eyelids. "It must be nice," she said, thin-lipped.

Lucy threw back her head and laughed. "I don't mean those kinds of riches, child. Oh, goodness no! I mean riches that come from the earth. I've got a cow named Buttercup who feeds me milk and cream, an old mule named LaFayette who'll take me anywhere I please, a henhouse full of cackling Rhode Island Reds, good layers all, and a garden full of God's bounty."

Summer sipped her tea and didn't comment. The woman was entirely too happy.

"I'll fetch the gift I brought you," Lucy said and rose to walk to the wagon. She climbed into the back, rummaged around a bit, then with a chuckle stood up and waved a small bundle. "Here it is! I knew I hadn't lost it." She stepped from the wagon bed, onto the bench seat, then to the ground. "Wait till you see this!" She hurried back to the porch and unfolded the square cloth, her face aglow.

Lucy waited expectantly as Summer stared into the face of a wooden creature that stared back with unblinking intensity. For a moment Summer didn't speak, mostly because she didn't know what to say. The way Lucy was beaming, the thing was obviously a treasure.

Lucy sat down on the porch again. "My big brother Stephen gave it to me. It's one of my most treasured possessions."

"If it's special to you, why are you giving it to me?"

Lucy's smile gentled. "It's my gift for your baby. Something to make your little one real to you." She looked out at the horizon as if lost in thought. "You carry a precious life. You mention your condition from time to time, but usually it's because you're seeking something for yourself."

Summer flushed and started to argue the point, then fell quiet, knowing Lucy's words were true.

Lucy turned to her again. "Your child...this one who is bone of your bones, flesh of your flesh, is God's gift. Whenever you look at this doll, remember this little one you carry. Think of her dainty toes and fingers...or his yellow hair, the same ripe wheat color as yours. Imagine your child playing with this doll. Listen for your little girl's voice singing this doll a lullaby." She laughed lightly. "Or listen for the gruffer one of your sons as he tells you boys don't play with dolls."

Summer studied the doll's face and then touched its smooth

wooden cheek with her fingertips. "Did you name her? When you were a little girl, I mean?"

Lucy laughed again. "Oh, I tried out several, but none would stick. I knew she'd belonged to someone before me, and I used to worry myself silly that I wouldn't pick the right name. So I called her Honey, the same thing my papa used to call me."

"Well, Honey," Summer said, wondering at the sting behind her eyes, "you've just found yourself a new home." She raised her eyes to Lucy. "Thank you," she whispered. "Thank you."

Oregon–California Trail
Early Summer 1857

Sarah's papa swept her into his arms and settled her onto the saddle in front of him. They rode for a while until they were out ahead of the wagon train. He halted the tall horse by an outcrop of huge boulders. The sky was bigger than Sarah had ever seen before, and the land stretched out like Grandma's counterpane back home.

"Way over there, Sweet Pea, is the California Road. We'll be heading north for a ways, then due west."

Sarah nodded. She knew west was where they were going. West to California. "How much longer till we get there, Papa?"

He chuckled, and she enjoyed the rumble from his deep chest. "It's only May, and we've got weeks and weeks of travel ahead."

Since she lost Phoebe, it seemed both Ma and Pa—and even Meggie—were trying hard to spend time with her. She cried herself to sleep every night for a week after the crossing, and now it still hurt to think of her dolly floating down the river. She must be nearly out to sea by now. Meggie had told her so.

When Pa turned the big horse around, it danced sideways a bit. "I want you to stay close to Ma tonight," Pa said, squinting back toward the wagon company. "Will you do that for me?"

"Why, Papa?"

He studied the encampment and nudged the Appaloosa to a walk, then to a trot. "There's Pawnee trailing just behind us," he said. "Stragglers, most likely. But you stay close to Ma, hear me?"

It seemed her pa was always worrying over this thing or that, crossings and storms and making the nooning by high sun. Now Indians coming too close. She sighed and nodded. "I will, Papa."

Later, when Pa lifted her down from the saddle, she fixed her mind on the small band of Pawnees setting up camp just beyond the wagon circle while little children played and shouted nearby. Sometimes they turned to watch her, just as she was watching them.

She inched closer, wondering what it would be like to see a real Indian close up.

CHAPTER SEVEN

Summer placed the doll where she could see it from wherever she was working each day. It stood in the garden when she pulled weeds, in a small broken rocker while she scrubbed the floors and kitchen cabinets, and on a box as she tried to make a cradle out of some scraps of wood she found in the shed out back.

"Lucy said to imagine you with my little daughter or son," she said to Honey one evening as the sun faded into a hazy sunset. They were sitting on the top step of the porch stairs. "I'm finding that's hard to do, because I want my baby to have a papa." Tears stung her eyes, but this time they weren't for her. They were for her baby. She leaned back, thinking of Eli.

"Your papa would have been a good father, you know," she said to the doll. "Truly, the man is a saint. He must be, to have put up with the likes of me."

Sighing deeply, she stood and walked over to the rail, looking down the road, missing her husband more than ever. What she wouldn't give to see him walking down the dusty road, heading home, a jaunty smile on his face. Just like the smile he used to have for her, nearly melting her heart with those warm, gray eyes. Taking her into his arms, just as he once did beside the sea. It wouldn't even matter if the sea was a hundred miles away. It was his arms she missed.

"How long has it been since he looked at me that way?" Summer whispered to Honey as she sat down again. She cuddled the wooden doll, sorrow flowing into the deepest place in her heart for how she had treated her husband.

Days turned into weeks and weeks into months, and still Summer wept as she worked to prepare the house for the coming child. Her tears no longer welled up out of pity for her circumstances. Now they overflowed with sorrow for the pain she had caused her husband. She had shooed him off as surely as she had shooed off scraggly hens from her garden.

Summer poured out her faults to the doll, naming them one by one, feeling their burden press on her heart as if harsh words and selfish actions had happened only an hour ago. All those things she'd done to hurt others seemed to settle like a stagnant pool inside her.

One bright morning, Summer woke with a plan. "Honey," she announced to the doll, which lay by her side, "we're going to visit Lucy today. She's always heading down the road to visit us. I'm of a mind to bake a cake, and we'll take it to her."

She swung her feet over the side of the bed, and stood, only to fall back again as a stinging tightness spread through her abdomen. Puzzled, she waited until it subsided, then tried to stand once more. She had taken only a few steps, when another sharp pain took her breath away.

Lord, have mercy. She remembered the words from her childhood prayer book. *Christ, have mercy.* Summer crawled back to the bed and curled sideways, holding the doll tight. "It's not time," she wept. "Oh, my little one, it's too early. Don't come. Not yet."

She rubbed her stomach, willing the child to hear her voice. "I want you to be healthy and strong." A stronger contraction overtook her, and as it passed she wiped her tears, wondering what she should do to prepare for the birth. She lifted her head from the pillow, intending to put the kettle on to boil. But the effort was too much.

"Oh, Lucy," she whispered, "feel the nudging of need in your heart. Please come help me." Ashamed of her selfishness, she cried, "Please, come and help my baby."

Another painful tightness spread through her from inside out. *Lord, have mercy. Christ, have mercy.* She clutched Honey to her heart, taking comfort in the doll's wooden solidness.

When the next spasm hit, she drifted as if in a slow whirl into darkness. In the strange world between dreaming and pain and sorrow and terror, she imagined Lucy's voice. She imagined the feel of a cool cloth on her hot skin. But when she reached for the phantom fingers touching her forehead, she caught a very real hand in hers.

She wanted it to be Eli's. "Forgive me," she sobbed. "Forgive me for shooing you away."

A soft voice spoke, and she knew it wasn't Eli who stood near her. "Forgiveness isn't mine to give, child, for you've done me no harm. It's God you need to talk to, plain and simple, the way you've been speaking to Honey."

"How did you know?" Summer whispered, thinking she still might be dreaming.

"You haven't stopped talking to her, all this time." Once more, the cool touch on her forehead calmed her.

"My baby?" Summer whispered. "Is she all right?"

"Rest, child," the soft voice said. "Just rest."

Summer drifted again into the darkness. A great river of regret flowed through her, whirled around her, and deepened her fear. *Lord, have mercy. Is it too late for forgiveness? From Eli? From you? Christ, have mercy!*

A Presence as tender as a mama's lullaby, as strong as a cathedral full of voices singing of love and light and joy, surrounded Summer, filled her, lifted her above the dark river until it was no more.

Lord, have mercy. The Presence carried her as if with arms of love, a love more solid than anything she'd ever felt before. *Christ, have mercy.*

So this is what it's like to die, she realized with joy. Then she remembered. "I can't go yet. Not yet," she cried out. "Not yet." *The child...my baby...Eli's baby.* "I can't go!"

"Child, you're not going anywhere," Lucy said from somewhere nearby. She chuckled softly. "It will be a good long while before you can get up and around."

Summer forced her eyes open. Lucy bent over her and smiled gently. "Welcome back."

"The baby?"

"Your baby is fine, as tiny a tyke as I've ever seen but healthy as a horse."

"Can I see her?"

"Her?" Lucy laughed as she plumped Summer's pillows. "Child, you've got yourself a fine little boy."

"A son?" Summer smiled weakly. "Imagine that. A son."

Lucy stepped toward the door, looking as joyous as Summer had ever seen her. "Are you up to seeing him?"

Summer nodded. "Yes ma'am. I can't wait another minute." She closed her eyes and imagined the color of his hair…if he had any, the slope of his cheek, the shape of his eyes, the soft pink of his ears. With a sigh, she settled deeper into the pillows, praying for the strength to hold him, even once, before sleep overtook her again.

"Here he is," Lucy said softly.

When Summer opened her eyes, it wasn't Lucy who was holding her son.

She swallowed hard, feeling the sting of tears behind her eyes. "Eli?" she whispered, afraid to believe.

His tears matched hers. He hesitated for only a heartbeat before bringing their son to her. Eli sat on the edge of her bed, then tenderly, so tenderly, placed the bundle in her arms. Her husband's gentle gray eyes met hers, then he watched as she folded back the corner of the flannel blanket to peer with wonder into their son's face.

"He's beautiful," she breathed.

Eli's hands brushed hers as he helped her unwrap the baby. "You made a beautiful baby," he said, meeting her eyes again.

"We did," she said, "together."

Nate McKenzie was four years old when he found a pretty hatbox tucked in a corner of his mother's wardrobe. It was on the top shelf, so he had to scoot a chair nearby, then reach high to pull the hatbox from the shelf by a ribbon tied around it. The chair teetered, and he hollered as he fell to the wooden floor with a clatter and a bang. The sound of his yelp brought the household running: his ma, who'd recently had his baby brother; his pa, who had just come home from his new tractor store in town; and his nanny, Miz Lucy, who was the first to reach him.

"Well now, fancy this," she said, spotting the hatbox, resting upside down beside him. "Whatever did you find?" She wore a secret smile, as if she knew the contents might be special somehow.

Before he could ask, his mother crowded in to stoop beside him. She frowned as she checked his limbs the way she always did when he tumbled, to make sure they worked. "You shouldn't have climbed high like this, especially on a teetery chair. You could have been hurt."

Though her words were sharp, they didn't match the gentle look in her eyes. She cuddled him close and kissed the top of his head. "You take care now," she said. "You ask me next time you need help."

"Sometimes you're too busy," he said.

Pa stood nearby, holding Nate's little brother against his shoulder to get him to burp. "You mind your ma now, son."

"Yes sir." Nate stood and brushed himself off. Then he noticed his ma and his nanny were bent over the hatbox, unwrapping something. They smiled at each other as Nanny lifted a wooden doll into her arms.

"Well now," she said, pleased, "I believe it's our little Honey."

Nate knelt beside her as she examined the toy.

"This doll's been to war. Let me show you." The boy crept closer as Nanny lifted the doll's faded calico dress. "This was made by a bullet—this spot here. It was just grazed."

Nate ran his finger along the long spiral bullet mark, then he narrowed his eyes for a closer inspection. His gaze lit on the whittle marks, the face, the carved curly hair. "It's for girls," he said, wrinkling his nose. He handed it back to Nanny. "It's got a dress and girl's hair."

Nanny met his mama's gaze, their eyes bird-bright as they looked at each other. "I have an idea," Nanny said, looking down at the doll. "I do believe—with a stitch here, a stitch there—this little wooden doll would make a fine toy soldier."

Nate expelled his breath in a low whistle. "A real soldier?"

"It's already been to war. I think it only fitting."

Nate wrapped his arms around his nanny's neck. "How soon? I want it now!"

"All good things come in their own time," his ma said from across the room. "It's God's way."

Then his pa did the silliest thing. Standing right there, leaning against the doorjamb while he burped the baby, Pa bent over and kissed Ma right on the lips.

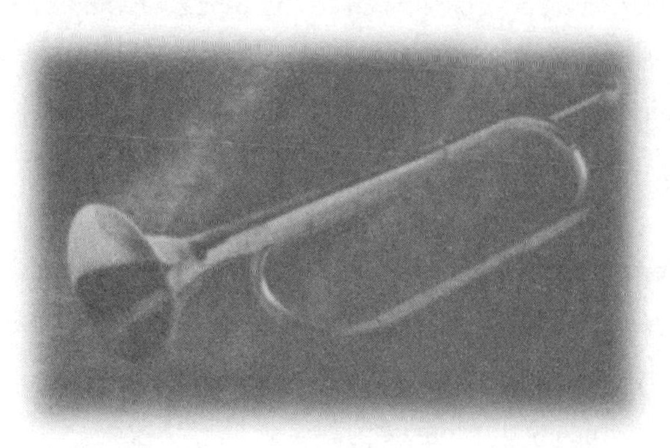

"Mama," Sarah said, "that little black-eyed girl keeps watching us." The Indians had set up camp next to the circled wagon company just minutes after Pa halted his group. The Pawnee mas and pas had laid out their wares to trade on blankets while the children played noisily, shouting and laughing and carrying on, just as Sarah and Meggie and their friends did.

All except for the little black-eyed girl about Sarah's size, only scrawnier. She sat by her ma, silent as all get-out, staring wide-eyed at Sarah and Meggie.

Her hand in a pot-mitt, Mama carried a griddle from the cookfire to the back of the wagon and set it down to cool.

"She looks hungry," Meggie said, her eyes still fixed on the black-eyed girl. "Maybe she'd like some johnnycake."

"I think she wants to play with us," Sarah said in amazement.

Mama laughed. "How about taking some johnnycake to the little girl and her mother?" She smiled at the twins. "I want you to come right back, but you can smile friendlylike while you're there."

Sarah was the first to jump up and head to the griddle. She touched the cake with her fingertips. "It's cooled, Mama. I want to carry it."

"Huh-uh," Meggie said, crowding close to Sarah, "I get to. I was the first one to say they look hungry."

"Huh-uh," Sarah said, "I was the first one to say they want to play."

"Girls!" Ma said sternly. "Neither of you will carry it if you don't quit your wrangling this minute."

Sarah's bottom lip pooched out before she could stop it. Ma spotted it, raised an eyebrow, and placed the johnnycake loaf in Meggie's hands. The girls headed toward the Pawnee camp, and Sarah's heart danced at the very thought of such an adventure. Their mama stood by the wagon, watching.

The black-eyed girl looked up as they approached. Her face was round and kind, and Sarah smiled. Then she saw what the little girl held in her arms.

"Phoebe!" she hollered and grabbed her doll. "My Phoebe!"

But quick as a wink the Pawnee girl snatched the doll away from Sarah. By now the rest of the Indian camp had fallen silent. Sarah let out another howl, bringing her papa running. He gathered up Sarah and Meggie in his arms and headed back to the wagon circle.

"Phoebe," Sarah cried, looking over Pa's shoulder at her doll, cradled in the Pawnee girl's arms. "Phoebe!"

CHAPTER EIGHT

Temecula, California
1862

It was past midnight when the household finally fell quiet. Fourteen-year-old Stephen Ward climbed from his bed, pulled on his overalls and brogans, and then crept from the bedroom he shared with his five brothers. Making sure he missed every creaking board, he tiptoed by his parents' room, then past the small room where his little sister, Lucy, slept. Somehow the child sensed he was there, creeping down the hallway.

She was his favorite of the passel, but she could be a caution. Like now. "Stephen?" she whispered loudly. "That you?"

He stepped to her doorway. "It's me, pumpkin. You go back to sleep."

"Where you going?" Lucy yawned loudly.

"Just outside. Nowhere special. You go back to sleep now."

Stephen had made his way nearly to the front door when he heard the floor creak behind him. He halted midstep, but before he turned around, he knew it was Lucy.

"I want to go too." She was standing in a bar of light from

the moon shining through a nearby window. When she took his hand and gazed up at him, adoration was written on her sweet round face.

"You can't, pumpkin."

"Why?"

"I'm going off someplace where you can't come. But it's a secret. No one else knows."

Her eyes opened wide. "Nobody?"

"Only you."

"Ma and Pa don't know?"

"I'll write and tell them later, but for now"—he knelt beside her—"it's our secret. Promise me you won't tell?"

After a short pause, she nodded. "When are you comin' back home? Tomorrow?"

"Nobody expects the war to last long, so I'll be home before you know it."

"You're goin' to war?"

"Joining up with the Massachusetts regiment, just like all Californians who want to help preserve the Union." He felt proud saying it.

"But Ma and Pa, they said you couldn't." She watched him now with dark, solemn eyes. "They said you're too young. I remember them sayin' it."

He straightened up tall and squared his shoulders. "I look more than fourteen. I look at least sixteen. Everybody says so."

Lucy looked ready to cry. "Pa'll skin you alive for lyin'. I know he will." Her lower lip quivered. "He says if there's one thing he can't abide, it's lyin'. He says it's near as bad as killin'."

"That's why you can't tell, pumpkin. Let me be on my way, so's Pa can't catch me." He chuckled softly. "You wouldn't want me to get skinned alive, would you?"

She shook her head. "No sir."

"You do as I say, and everything will be all right. You'll see." He moved to the door. Then he turned for one last look. Lucy was crying, and it nearly broke his heart. He stooped down once more and gave her a big bear hug. "I'll be home quicker than you can shake a stick."

She swiped at her watery eyes with her fists, then looked up at him wordlessly. Unable to bear his little sister's sorrow, Stephen opened the door and stepped outdoors before he could change his mind. He'd packed his kit days earlier and hid it in the hollow trunk of a dead oak tree out back. He pulled it out and slung it over his shoulder, then set off down the road to town.

The moon was high, and his spirits lifted. He was off to fight in a glorious war. This was no time for sorrow or regrets. Someday when he came home, it would be to honor and glory. His ma and pa would praise his actions.

He puffed out his chest just thinking about it. Then they would understand. They likely wouldn't even mind the money he'd stolen for stagecoach fare from his ma's sugar jar in the pantry. Though right now he'd likely get a licking if they found out.

As he strode along the road in the moonlight, he pushed any

twinges of regret to the back of his mind. It helped to think about the adventure ahead: the glories of wearing the fine uniform of the Ninth Massachusetts, shooting a rifle, and galloping across the battlefield on a tall and splendid horse. He did have some doubts about the horse but didn't let those stop him from dreaming.

The stagecoach was due to leave for Yuma at noon, so when Stephen reached town he hid behind a clump of manzanita, waiting for Ned to join him. The boys had been friends since they were knee-high to skeeterbugs and had planned such an adventure for nearly as long.

By and by, Ned slipped into the scrub brush beside Stephen. "Anybody see you?" He swept a clump of red hair from his eyes, looking scared and excited at the same time.

"Just Lucy. She was cryin' when I left."

Ned sighed. "I got all goosepimply when I lit out, thinking Ma might of spied me through her window. She's known for almost having second sight about her young uns." He shrugged. "But nobody followed, so I'm figuring we're safe."

"You bring your gear?"

Ned grinned and patted his rucksack. "Got it."

"Money?"

His face fell. "Felt terrible about that part. Stealing and all."

"It's for a good cause," Stephen assured him. "How about the bugle?"

Ned rocked back on his heels, looking confident again. "Got

up in the attic last night. Found it in Grampa's trunk—just where I'd seen it last."

Stephen grinned and slapped Ned on the back the way he'd seen menfolk do. "Now all you gotta do is learn how to blow it. Just keep thinking of the glory of leading the troops with your bugling."

The morning birds were beginning to sing now that the sun was up, and a breeze rustled the live oak branches overhead. It was an altogether fine day for going off to war.

"You going to buy the fares?" Ned asked when the Butterfield stage office opened.

Stephen narrowed his eyes, measuring the distance that they'd be in the open, increasing their chances of being recognized. "Ain't a good idea to wait till later," he said. "More folks that know us'll be coming into town."

"I'll go then." Ned stood and brushed off his pants. When he reached for Stephen's coins, his hands were shaking.

"You skeered?" Stephen didn't want to admit his own insides were jumpy as treefrogs.

"Nah," Ned said with a shrug. And off he trotted to the Butterfield counter, his hands in his pockets, his skinny elbows stuck out like chicken wings.

A stagecoach had just halted alongside the Butterfield office, team snorting and wagon creaking, when a passel of little girls scampered from the back of a farm wagon.

Stephen nodded toward the little uns as soon as Ned got back. "Think they're going to be aboardin' with us?"

"Their ma and pa are heading into the mercantile. Likely just brought everyone along for the ride." A glimmer of something sad darkened his eyes, and he turned away from the scene.

But Stephen watched as two girls, alike enough to be twins with their pigtails and freckled noses, twirled and jumped on and off the wooden walkway in front of the Butterfield station. While a fresh team was being hitched to the stagecoach, their little sister scampered nearby. She cradled a doll, chattering and singing to it as she hopped inside the stagecoach and played until her sisters called to her to come out.

She skipped toward the mercantile, hand in hand with her sisters, at the same time their ma and pa came through the swinging doors, loaded down with sacks and bushel baskets. Soon the children passed back and forth through the double doors, helping their parents carry sacks of flour and sugar and coffee and grain to their wagon.

Something about the scene made the back of Stephen's throat smart as he thought about his family doing the same thing, just as they always had, every Monday morning. Only he wouldn't be with them. From the corner of his eye, he saw Ned swipe at his runny nose.

The stagecoach driver headed to the fresh team and checked the tack while passengers milled about, waiting to board. Stephen poked Ned as both boys scanned the street. With a nod of agreement, they moved from their hiding place, trotted to the stage, and climbed in. Settling against the horsehair bench, Stephen slumped to avoid being seen through the open window. Ned sat opposite him, looking glum. Stephen didn't want to ask his friend if he'd changed his mind. He was afraid of the answer.

As the other passengers began to board, Stephen swallowed hard and glanced across at Ned to see how he was faring. But the boy had his eyes closed, either because he was praying or he was about to be sick.

He looked back to the family with longing while the other passengers crowded into the coach, settled onto the bench seats, and chattered about the journey ahead. The driver closed the door and climbed to the seat up top, where he popped the reins and yelled, "Gee-yup!"

The stage lurched forward, swaying and bumping along the dusty road. As it began rounding the corner at the smithy's, he heard hollering and looked back. The little girl was crying in the middle of the road and rubbing her eyes. She reminded him of Lucy, and he turned away before his own tears could embarrass him in front of the other passengers. After all, he was a soldier now. Goin' off to war, he was, and soldiers didn't cry.

The driver wasn't letting any grass grow under his team. The town soon disappeared behind them in a cloud of dust.

With a sigh, Stephen slumped against the seat and closed his eyes, thinking of the adventure ahead. He wasn't sure how much time had passed when he jerked awake and rubbed his eyes, but the sun was round and high. With a loud yawn, he looked up, startled to see the inside of a coach filled with other slumbering passengers. He'd been dreaming of home and was surprised not to find himself in his bed.

He yawned again and sat up, ready to give Ned a gentle kick on the calf to wake him.

It was then he noticed the doll. It was propped in the corner of the coach below Ned, staring out at the world as if embarking on a grand adventure. He reached for it, thinking about the little girl and her cries as they left town.

He turned it over in his hands, wondering how he might return it when he didn't even know the family's name. They might have been just passing through.

Then it struck him, and he smiled.

Well now, he thought, *the whole town will turn out when Ned and me come back heroes, all triumphant-like. Maybe the little girl and her family will be there. Likely there'll be a parade. And when they're presentin' us with medals at the bandstand, we'll tell the little girl her dolly brought us luck, helped us win, and she'll be proud as punch to have a dolly that's been in this great and glorious conflict.*

He stuck the wooden doll in his rucksack. Then, settling back into the corner, he closed his eyes again and thought about the trip ahead: stage to Yuma, horseback to Santa Fe, freight wagon to St. Louis, and train to Massachusetts, where all able-bodied California men were joining Abe Lincoln's great army.

Able-bodied men. As the stagecoach rounded another corner, Stephen swayed with the vehicle and grinned. *Me and Ned are men going off to war.*

In the back of the wagon, under the hooped canvas cover, Sarah lay on her pallet bed. Her heart squeezed tight each time she thought of the little black-eyed girl cradling Phoebe, hugging her close.

From outside the wagon, Ma and Pa's voices drifted toward her. Her pa talked of bargaining with the Pawnee, trading them for the doll. But her ma said, "It's not the right thing to do, Alexander. The little girl loves Phoebe as much as Sarah does. She would be left with empty arms."

"That's why I love you so much, Ellie," Sarah's pa said. "The way you care so about others, not just our family, but others. Like the Pawnee child." He fell quiet for a while, and Sarah heard only the night sounds, the frogs and crickets and owls. Then Pa said, "I know getting Phoebe back seems a small thing, considering all that lies ahead."

"But your little girl's heart is broken."

"Yes," he said, nearly too low for Sarah to hear. "I won't always be around to comfort her when her heart breaks, but when I am here—like now—there should be something I can do."

Sarah sat up in bed, listening for what Pa would say next.

But it was her ma who spoke. "What a sorrowful thought."

"Once we're in California and Sarah grows up, marries, and has babies of her own, I won't always be there. At least, not the same way I am now—to kiss a skinned knee or wipe away a tear."

Her parents' voices dropped to a soft whisper in the night, mixing with the chorus of night song.

Babies of my own? Sarah lay back down on her bed and stared up at the canvas cover. With a deep sigh, she fell asleep at last, dreaming of a cradle full of babies all as pretty as Phoebe.

But even so, her arms ached for the one she couldn't have.

CHAPTER NINE

Gettysburg, Pennsylvania
1863

The war wasn't a glorious affair at all. For half a year Stephen had tramped with the Massachusetts Ninth, acting as groom for the officers' horses. Ned had blown his bugle when called upon. They'd seen the fighting from a distance. Until today.

This was the first time he'd gone into battle with a musket in his hands, and he was trembling from his shoulders to his boots. His finger shook so bad he surely couldn't squeeze the trigger. He'd been taken over by the nervous shakes since noon, when after too many had fallen, he was ordered to pick up the musket from a fallen soldier and fall in with the Ninth at Peach Orchard.

Stephen blinked back his tears as he held the musket level, sighting down the barrel at the troops coming over the ridge. He was on his belly, in a gully shaped like a grave. As he watched the men leap over the hill, he spotted monarch butterflies and bees in the grass, and off yonder, a yellow dog nosing about the ground might have been tracking a gopher. The sight made him cry harder.

"Stay back," he shouted at the Rebs. "Go on now. Go back. Please, stay back!" His tears made the sight shimmer like heat waves on hot California sand. Mixed with the flowers and butterflies, the oncoming soldiers looked like a kaleidoscope he'd seen once at the fair.

Then a regiment of Rebs rose above the ridge, standing straight and tall and close enough for Stephen to see. He sighted in on a foot soldier with hair as bright as the sun, straight as corn silk. He was as pale as Ma's flour jar and looked about as scared as Stephen felt.

"Fire," shouted Captain Birney from down the line. "Fire, now!"

Fire? But the Reb is only a boy, not much older than me. Swallowing hard, Stephen squeezed back on the trigger. But not all the way. His shoulder ached from holding the musket tight and not firing. His hand still shook something fierce.

"You don't shoot, he'll git you first, sure as anythin'," he heard Ned call out from three men down. "You don't go getting yourself shot now, Stephen Ward. You shoot, hear me? You shoot!" It was Ned's first time too, and Stephen wondered if he was crying and saying things to his best friend that he should be saying to himself.

What if that Reb boy shoots Ned?

Stephen blinked the water from his eyes and found his target again. Weeping, he squeezed the trigger all the way. The bright-haired boy slumped and clutched his side.

In the confusion of battle, the sounds of cannon fire and musket balls flying, the shouts, the blood, the cries, Stephen crept low toward the Reb. Around him, the air was alive with fragments of exploding shells and splinters torn from mangled trees. The boy looked up at Stephen with fear, his face as dirty as soot.

"I'll git you outta here," Stephen said, feeling he had found some purpose in the terror of the day. "Where're you hurt?"

"Here," the child said, "Here on my side." He lifted his arm and showed Stephen the gaping hole.

"Hold onto me now," Stephen said, laying down his musket and picking up the boy. "Swing your good arm around my neck."

Around them swirled the noise and dust and cries. The smoke from the muskets and cannons and rifles hung so muddy and thick, not a soul paid any mind to what they were doing or where they were headed.

The Reb did as he was told, and Stephen helped him limp to a stand of splintered oaks. "You stay here till you're found." He laid the boy's head against a gnarled oak trunk. "When some Reb who's not crazy with shootin' comes around, you holler out for help, you hear?"

Behind them the sounds of artillery thundered, and the cries continued. Stephen sat down beside the Reb. "What's your name?"

The boy managed a weak smile. "Eddie Johnson. What's yours?"

"Stephen Ward. All the way from California."

"This ain't your war." The boy didn't sound convinced that it was his either. He closed his eyes.

Stephen drew himself up and declared, "I'm fighting to save the Union. Mister Lincoln's Union."

The boy laughed softly, but it came out a gurgling sound. "We're just boys, you and me. Should be playing at home in our swimming holes and such. I'd give near about anything right now to swing from an old willow branch and drop like a cannonball into the water." He opened his eyes. "You got a creek back home?"

Stephen grinned, feeling good about relating it. "Swim there with my brothers and sister. There's a whole passel of 'em." He chuckled, thinking of them all, the boys and Lucy and his promise to come right home. "Good trout fishing, too. I'd catch enough to feed the family, bring 'em home for Ma to fry up."

The boy's eyes were closed again, and his breathing had turned shallow. When Eddie coughed, Stephen put an arm around his shoulders, feeling a sting behind his eyes. Half a year ago, he'd never seen anybody die. Now he'd seen plenty, but never someone in his arms. Never someone he shot. He wondered if Eddie knew it was him who did it.

"Why'd you come after me?" Eddie asked, his eyes still closed.

"I-I don't know. I suppose it was because I saw you fall, saw you needed help."

Their eyes met, and Stephen saw the boy didn't know it was

Stephen who shot him. "I would have done the same, you know," Eddie said.

"Helped me?"

Eddie didn't answer. Behind them cannon boomed, rockets whistled, shells exploded. The ground shook with volley after volley.

"Will you post a letter to my ma?" the boy finally whispered. "Here, in my pocket. I kept it for such a time, hoping there'd be somebody to send it."

"Yes sir, I will," Stephen promised. "And I'll tell her you're a hero. I'll write her this very night and tell her."

Eddie laughed, causing him to cough again. "She might wonder at such words coming from a Yankee."

"Nevertheless, I'll do it. I'll find a way. I know what it would mean to my ma to hear such a thing." He laughed bitterly. "I don't know about you, but when I headed off to war, I thought it a glorious thing. But now, after all I've seen, the death…the sorrow…there's no more glory at all."

Eddie's stillness caused Stephen to look down. The boy had stopped breathing. "Don't die," Stephen whispered, knowing it easily could have been him. Or Ned or a thousand others this day.

It *was* a thousand others just like Eddie. Thousands, maybe. They lay out on the battlefield, right now, dying. Stephen hung his head, wondering how he'd ever thought war anything but shameful.

By dusk, the battlefield had turned into a tangle of bodies. The mud ran red, and the cries of the wounded pierced the smoke-filled air.

"I've got to find me a post office," he said to Ned that night as they were bedding down in their tent.

"Around here?"

"I've got myself something to mail..." He let his voice fall off, unwilling to tell of the Reb dying in his arms. Besides, he was half thinking about not returning. Just ridding himself of his uniform and hightailing west. He was ashamed to tell Ned his thoughts.

"You writing home?"

Stephen didn't answer. He wanted to write Ma and Pa, but he feared they wouldn't forgive him for what he'd done. And he was haunted by the face of the little girl missing her doll. There would be no parade down the dusty main street of town for the heroes' return. It was doubtful they'd go home at all, though he'd never say so to Ned.

"The doll... It's the doll," he lied, thinking that might satisfy his friend's curiosity. "I need to send it back. I always figured we'd take it back in person. But after what we've seen, I wonder..." He couldn't finish, thinking of the Reb boy taking his last breath while resting his head in the crook of Stephen's arm.

"I'll go with you then, if that's what you're up to."

"Nah. I'll be back in a flash. Just want to hightail it into town.

I hear it's only a few miles yonder." He just wanted to get away from the battle, he didn't care about anything more. He'd seen too much blood. He couldn't bear it another day.

"Ain't that against the rules?" Ned's eyes were round. "I thought we couldn't leave."

"This is important." He pulled the doll out of the rucksack and turned it over in his hands. "If there's a court-martial, it'll only be for me. You need to stay."

Ned rolled on his side so that he was facing Stephen. "Knowing you were down the line from me yesterday, well, that helped me through it all." He shrugged. "If you wasn't here, it'd be harder to fire. When you disappeared today…well, I ducked out. Hid till it was over. Wish they'd take me back as bugle boy."

Stephen laughed to lighten the mood. "Maybe it'd help if you could carry a tune."

"That wasn't why they put a musket in my hands." Ned sounded scared. "That wasn't why they taught me how to squeeze the trigger."

Stephen nodded, thinking again how he owed it to Ned to tell him he was planning on deserting. But he couldn't form the words. He couldn't say how knowing he'd killed a boy had made him old inside. How he'd seen the very spirit of the child leave his body, and he'd been changed forever.

He felt the crying rise up from his chest, and he turned away from Ned so his friend couldn't see his struggle. "Same with me, Ned," he finally said. "That's why they put one in my hands. Told me to squeeze the trigger like I was in love with my musket, loved it like my girl back home. I didn't say I wasn't old enough to have a girl waiting for me."

Clamping his jaw so his chin wouldn't tremble, he flopped on his back again, staring at the top of the canvas tent. Sounds of the bivouac carried from outside: the creaking wagons still collecting the wounded, the moans and occasional screams drifting from the surgeon's quarters, mixed with the shoveling of mass graves and the nervous laughter of men closer in as they talked about the next day's battle and how they'd make sure they'd beat back Johnny Reb for sure this time. Stephen blinked back the sting from the cookfire smoke and the smell of death.

"You stay here, Ned," he finally said, the ache inside him twisting deeper. "I'll take that wooden doll to town."

The early morning sky was still tar black when Stephen rose and slipped from the tent. He'd buttoned his uniform coat over his shirt, planning to discard all signs of his soldiering as soon as he was away from the encampment. He didn't dare take his rucksack for fear it would be noticed that he was leaving for longer than a stroll in the woods, or for Ned to know he wasn't intending to return.

Supplies were kept at the rear of the encampment, and if anyone asked, he'd tell them his commanding officer had sent him. But no one paid him any mind. Wagons were being loaded with artillery, mess was being prepared, and surgeons were still sawing. The stench of blood mixed with smells of breakfast ham and corn mush. Fighting to keep his head clear and his stomach from lurching, he awaited his chance to mix with the other soldiers and slip away unnoticed.

As soon as he had sidled through a row of saplings, he dashed across a strip of meadow and into a deeper wood. The war lay behind him, farther away with each step, but the dread shame of killing lay like a stone in his heart.

He crashed through the woods, his face wet with sweat and tears, his breathing coming in pants, his chest rising and falling.

Then he heard a cartridge drop into a rifle chamber. The sound was unmistakable. He froze, afraid to draw another ragged breath. Not a bird twittered. Not a frog croaked. Not a leaf rattled in the breeze. Only dead silence, and the thunder of blood pounding in his ears.

At the same moment he heard a footfall behind him on the trail and the panting of another runner. His heart caught, then pounded still harder.

He turned to see who followed, curious but still conscious of the rifle likely pointed at him from the sapling thicket beyond the clearing.

"Stephen!" Ned yelled, coming into sight and holding up a bundle wrapped in canvas. The boy grinned as he trotted closer. "Here you run off to mail the thing and you forgot what you're up to." He laughed. "You been hightailin' it so fast I could hardly catch up. Bring you this." He held out the canvas wad. "Your ma always said you'd forget your head if it warn't attached."

He was but ten feet away from Stephen when the shot rang out. The thunder from it echoed and rumbled through the woods as Ned crumpled to the ground.

Sarah felt the touch of her mother's hand on her shoulder. She squeezed open her eyes, yawned, and blinked in the lantern light. "Is it time to get up already?"

Her mother's smile was wide. "Yes, child," she whispered then fell silent.

Sarah closed her eyes again. "I want to sleep longer." She turned over, shielding her face against the lantern. "It's too early, Mama."

"Maybe not today." Ma sounded like she couldn't stop smiling.

"It's always too early," Meggie whined, and Meggie never whined.

Then a queer scent drifted into Sarah's nostrils. She wrinkled her nose, and sniffed again. "What's that?" It smelled smoky, like a log that had been in the fire too long but not burnt all the way to embers.

Her ma laughed lightly. "Open your eyes, little one. See for yourself."

On the pallet beside Sarah's, Meggie sat up and yawned. "What is it?"

"We had a visitor last night," Ma said after she had kissed them each good morning. "Someone from the Pawnee camp."

Sarah's heart beat faster. She craned her neck to look back at her ma again. "Who?"

Ma didn't answer but her gaze dropped to something tucked in the pallet bed. Sarah looked down too, then gaped in wonder. "Phoebe?" she whispered. "Is it you?"

Beside her lay the doll, dirty and bedraggled. Her tattered clothes hung in shreds. But none of it mattered. Sarah covered the doll's smooth, worn face with kisses. "You're back," she whispered. "You came back!"

"I think she's spent a lot of time in the little Pawnee girl's arms by the cookfire," Ma said gently. "Maybe you can give her a bath, wash her clothes, before we break camp."

"The little black-eyed girl brought her back?" Meggie looked worried.

Their ma nodded. "Or someone from their band."

Without another word, Meggie scrambled to the back of the wagon, picked up the hatbox with Rosebud inside, and headed down the stairs.

Sarah and her ma stood at the canvas opening and watched as Meggie headed straight into the Pawnee camp. Dawn had broken, and it was just light enough to see the little black-eyed girl run to meet Meggie.

They sat down cross–legged on a Pawnee blanket. Meggie took off the hatbox lid, lifted out the doll, and placed it in the little girl's arms.

Ma smiled down at Pa, who was hitching the team to the wagon. They both seemed to have water in their eyes.

CHAPTER TEN

"Ned!" Stephen ducked below the gunfire and dove to where Ned lay. Sheltering Ned's body with his own, he lifted the musket and sighted down the barrel toward the stand of saplings.

There, hidden in the brush, a flash of a Reb's dirty gray uniform appeared in the V at the end of the barrel. He lifted his aim slightly, and a face came into view. The man narrowed his eyes as he raised his own rifle and prepared to fire again.

Stephen's shoulder went all atremble, and his fingers shook as he squeezed on the trigger. His insides threatened to heave, though he hadn't eaten for two days. He swallowed hard and thought about Ned's lifeless body behind him. The Reb had done it, but so had Stephen for deceiving his friend the way he did. What he'd done before was bad. Deceiving the folks at home. Stealing from his ma. Killing a boy. But Ned was his best friend in the world. Now he was gone.

The sound of another shell clacking home echoed through the wood. With a sob, Stephen closed his eyes, praying for forgiveness but wondering if it would ever be his. Then he squeezed the trigger. Slowly, just like he'd been taught.

The blast deafened him and sent him reeling backward, toppled up against Ned.

When the echo died, only silence remained. There was no sound of rustling in the brush. Only silence from Johnny Reb. Stephen was elated and scared all at once.

He sat quiet, not daring to move, and wondering if he should crawl over to the Reb. Make sure he was dead. But he imagined what the man might look like and was sick again.

Then he heard a chuckle from behind him, and the hair at the back of his neck stood on end. He turned to see Ned grinning at him. The boy was pale and shaking all over.

"You saved my life," Ned said weakly.

Stephen crawled over to Ned and frowned, looking down at where his friend had surely been hit. "You been pullin' my leg all this time? Playing like you're dead?" He didn't know whether to be mad as a wet hen or cry with relief.

"I *thought* I was dead." Ned tried to sit up, then groaned and fell back. "I been hit. Real bad, I think." He looked down curiously, felt his chest, and winced. "But there's no blood."

"I saw you go down. Thought you were a goner for sure."

"I thought we both were." Ned laughed. "Till you took care of Johnny Reb." He nodded toward the thicket. "He was after us both."

"He's beyond the lines. Shouldn't of been here. This far out." Stephen stared toward the place where he was certain the body lay.

"Maybe he slipped behind 'cause he was a spy or something."

"Or maybe because he was runnin' too." Stephen let his gaze drift away from his friend's face.

Ned groaned as he sat up. "That's what you were adoin'? Runnin'?"

"I seen too much of all this. Shot this boy yesterday, and he died on me. Sitting right there as close as you are. Told me about his ma and pa, and we talked about our brothers and sisters. He talked about his swimming hole and asked about ours. Said neither of us belonged in this war, and I thought the same." Stephen was crying now and still looking off in the woods. "I promised I'd mail his ma a letter, and that's what I lit out to do. Then I got to thinkin' that I'd just keep running."

"I've thought the same thing, time to time," Ned said quietly. It sounded as if he was looking off in the distance too, and his voice trembled as if he was as close to bawling as Stephen had been all morning.

"You want to keep going?" Stephen turned back to look him in the face. Around them the birds were twittering up a storm, and the forest bugs were skittering and flying, and the earth seemed to be coming to life again. "Keep running, I mean?"

"Nah." Ned groaned as he bent forward to brush himself off. "I'll do what they tell me, and I'll think about Mister Lincoln and what this is all about. It ain't the glory anymore. It's something deeper." He laughed softly. "Leastwise, that's what I've been telling myself."

"What about the killin'?" Stephen stood and reached for Ned's hand to help him to his feet. "You're not worried about it?

That it may go on, all the killing?" He didn't say it, but he knew they both were thinking that every bullet or cannon shot could be the one meant for them.

Ned met his eyes, and it seemed to Stephen that it was a man looking back at him, not a thirteen-year-old boy. There was a sorrow, a knowing, a wisdom, even a hardness that he hadn't seen before. He wondered if it was the same in his own eyes.

Stephen nodded. "I'm going back too." He bent over and reached for the bundle of wooden doll and canvas wrapping that had fallen to the ground.

With a groan, Ned moved to have a look at the dead Johnny Reb, but Stephen stared at the wad of canvas in his hands. The bullet meant for Ned had hit the cover, tearing a ragged, singed hole through it.

Stephen whistled under his breath as he removed the cover. The little wooden doll stared up at him. Her dress was torn open from where the bullet grazed, leaving a slice only as deep and wide as a sapling twig across her middle.

"Can you fancy that?" He turned the toy this way and that in wonder, then held it up for Ned to see as he limped back across the clearing. "I do believe God is with us after all."

Ned took the doll from Stephen and ran his hand over the place where it had taken the glancing strike from the bullet. "Never been any doubt," he said softly. "Never."

His eyes locked again with Stephen's, clear wisdom shining in them once more. Then he grinned. "And we're gonna need him more'n ever now. Here we are, comin' back in the midst of battle. If we're caught, we'll be shot for deserting on the spot."

"I'll take the blame for us both," Stephen said, wrapping one arm around Ned's shoulders as they began to tramp south.

Ned pulled aside a sapling for Stephen to pass. "You'd better. You got me into this. Was your idea to head to war."

Stephen laughed, feeling better than he had in days. "But you owe me, Ned. Case you forgot. I just saved your life."

"And just maybe you'll get that parade you wanted," Ned said, and then his voice turned serious. "But something tells me this war's not gonna be over quick as we thought."

That night Stephen pulled out a writing pad, sharpened his quill, dipped it in a pot of ink, and began to write. Things long hidden in his heart—his sorrows, his guilt, his terrors, his hopes and fears—poured out. He didn't put them all on paper. He couldn't. The whole of it would only bring deeper sorrow to those who would read his letters.

The following morning as the encampment was coming to life, Stephen wrapped Eddie's letter inside one of his own, tied both securely to the doll, and dropped the bundle into a canvas mailbag. He posted it at the mail bin outside the supply tent, then hurried back to fetch his musket and gear.

Ned was just waking. He grinned and nodded as if nothing

out of the ordinary had happened the day before that changed them both. He dragged his fingers through his shock of red hair and, dressed in his own blue uniform and soldier's cap, followed Stephen from their tent. After mess, both boys stood at attention, muskets in hand, to receive their morning's orders.

The bugle blew, the drums rolled in cadence, and Stephen and Ned moved out in formation, marching into battle.

Utah Territory
Summer 1860

The day was hot and dry. A crackling wind blew through southern Utah Territory, reminding Sarah of the same kind of day three years earlier, a day of sorrow and loss. The day her pa died and then her ma just hours later.

She pushed the memories from her mind and instead met her twin sister's smile. New happiness had come to them, greater joy than they could have imagined back then. And one of the greatest joys was their little sister, Fae. She had been born just before their ma died.

Fae plopped down on the worn, faded quilt and looked up at her sisters expectantly.

Hannah, their friend who had cared for them since their ma and pa died that day at Mountain Meadows, laughed and bent to kiss Fae on the top of her curly head. "Be patient, little Fae," she said, hugging the child. "Your sisters have a surprise for you." She reached into the picnic basket to fetch their lunch.

Sarah grinned. Fried chicken and corn bread as only Hannah could make them.

"What's my s'prise?" Fae wrinkled her nose.

Meg scooted closer on the quilt; she wore a knowing smile as if giving Phoebe to Fae had been all her idea. "Hurry," she said to Sarah. "I can't wait to see how Fae likes it."

"Well, first," Sarah said dramatically, "you need to know how special my present is." Little Fae bobbed her head up and down as Sarah continued. "This is something I would not give to just anyone. Only you."

Fae was up on her knees now, her eyes wide, watching as Sarah reached for Phoebe. But instead of handing her sister the doll, Sarah held Phoebe in her arms one last time, then kissed her on the forehead. She swallowed the sting in her throat and closed her eyes, feeling the solid warmth of the hardwood that her father had carved with such love.

She opened her eyes then, still staring at the faded face, the worn clothing, the whittling marks. "This is Phoebe," she said softly. She placed the doll in Fae's arms. "Our papa carved it with his own hands."

"And Mama made the clothes," Meg said. "New clothes after Phoebe spent time with the Indians." The twins exchanged glances above Fae's head as they remembered.

"It's a baby." Fae examined the doll's painted face with her finger.

"Phoebe," Sarah said. "Her name is Phoebe."

"Phoebe," repeated Fae, her forehead puckering as she tried out the new sound.

The little girl stared at the doll while the desert wind kicked up across the land, dust devils circled, and aspen rattled their dry leaves. The twins waited for Fae to speak. Finally, ignoring even the chicken drumstick Hannah held out to her, she hugged the doll tight.

"I love you," she whispered to Phoebe. "I will love you forever."

CHAPTER ELEVEN

Temecula, California
1864

Enid Ward shook out the children's wet clothes and pinned them one by one on the line that stretched from the back porch stairs to the outhouse. The sun was bright and warm with a stiff wind from the east. Though it was January, she expected her laundry to dry by sundown. She reached for another wooden pin and one of Charlie's socks. Wet clumps of the other boys' socks waited their turn. She knew whose they were by the sizes. Charlie was next oldest to Stephen, then came William, Theodore, Roger, and Thomas.

"Ma! Ma!" Lucy raced toward her as fast as her legs would carry her. She held a package, something that looked like a military mail-bag. "Ma!" she yelled, her cheeks bright. "Look what Pa just brought from town. Said it was in our mailbox at the mercantile."

Enid's husband, Albert, was only a few steps behind Lucy. "It's from our boy," he said, his voice gruff. "Posted from Gettysburg." The worry lines in his face were deeper than ever.

She dropped the stout wood pin along with William's socks,

and her hand fluttered to her heart. They had long since heard the news of the thousands who died in that battle. She fought to keep from crying in front of Lucy. "Gettysburg, so that's where our boy is," she said.

He nodded. "The address is written in his own hand, but he must have left there months ago."

"Let's open it!" Lucy jumped up and down, her pigtails bouncing. "Please, can we, can we?"

Enid was short of breath as she sat heavily on the top porch stair. She glanced at Albert's face, then looked back to Lucy. "Let your pa open it. It's only right."

With a shrug of disappointment, Lucy handed the heavy canvas bag to her father, then sat on one side of Enid as her father settled on the other. Enid clasped Lucy's hand in both of hers while Albert drew out the contents of the bag.

"Here it is," he said with a nod. "A letter—no, two, tied up with a doll."

Lucy gasped. "A dolly? For me?"

"Let's read the letter first, and we'll see," Albert said. And he began to read:

"Dear Ma and Pa and little uns,

"It seems nigh on to forever since I left. I learned myself a whole lot since I lit out. First of all, I'm sorry for the way I did it. I asked Lucy to keep a secret, and if she got in trouble for it, I'm sorry. It was my fault for talking her into it."

Albert stopped reading long enough to give a sharp glance to Lucy, then met Enid's gaze above her head.

"Go on," Enid said. She would deal with Lucy later about the secret she'd kept for more than a year.

He cleared his throat and began reading again.

"I'm sending with this letter a doll that was left on the Butterfield stagecoach the day I left. It belongs to a little un there in town. I don't know her name, but Ma, I figured maybe you could ask around for a family who's got twin girls with dark pigtails and another little un a few years younger.

"It was the littlest girl who left the doll on the stagecoach. She was crying to beat the band as we pulled away from the station. I always meant to bring it back myself someday, but now I know that may not happen for a long, long time. It may not happen at all.

"War is not what I thought it would be. But I still feel obliged to be fighting for a just cause, and for Mister Lincoln himself. I figure you might never welcome me home again after all I done, but even so I need to tell you how sorry I am for how I left. You deserved better from me. You deserved an honorable son, not someone playing at being a soldier and a hero. I've learned that it takes more than puffed-up pride to be a hero. It takes more than musket shootin' to be a soldier.

"I don't know if you can forgive me. Ma, every night I feel ashamed for the money I stole. You taught me better, but I forgot the lesson. Maybe it's not too late to learn.

"I'm in Pennsylvania at a place called Gettysburg. It was likely once a thing of beauty, with its meadow flowers and grand oaks, but now the beauty is gone. I can't tell you what remains.

"I remain,
"Your loving son,
"Stephen Ward

"P.S. If you can't find the girl the doll belongs to, please give it to Lucy. Tell her I have a yarn to tell about the bullet mark on the doll's middle. I'll save it till I get home and can tell it to her, face to face. There are words carved on the doll's back. It's worn so smooth I can hardly make it out. But it's something like this:

I WILL
LOVE YOU
4-EVER

"P.P.S. I'm sending two more letters inside this packet. Neither can be posted from our encampment. Could you send it to the address on top? The boy who gave it to me died in my arms. It didn't matter that he was the enemy. He was just a boy like me."

As Lucy took the doll in her hands, Albert met Enid's gaze and nodded, looking as though he might cry over his son's letter. No one spoke for several minutes. Not even Lucy, who studied the wooden doll, turning it this way and that in wonder.

Enid took the letter in her hands and held it to her face. Closing her eyes, she breathed in the musky scent of it, thinking her son had held it in his hands, had touched the paper with his fingers. She remembered those same chubby fingers grasping hers as Stephen took his first baby steps just fifteen years earlier. She remembered those hands playing patty-cake as his pa bounced him on his knee. She ran her fingertips over the laboriously scrawled, ink-smudged words: *You deserved an honorable son, not someone playing at being a soldier and a hero. I've learned that it takes more than puffed-up pride to be a hero. It takes more than musket shootin' to be a soldier.*

Enid studied the words and phrases, thinking only of how proud she was of him. Then she lifted a heart of thanksgiving to her Lord for such a son, who had learned life's hard lessons.

She looked back to Albert. "What about the other letters?"

"Both written to a family in Georgia. One in our son's writing, the other in someone else's."

A chill ran up Enid's spine, and she shuddered, thinking what it would be like to receive letters about her son's death. A mother on the other side of the continent was about to experience that deepest heart loss there could be. It didn't matter which side of the war she was on; this mother surely loved her son as much as Enid loved Stephen. How easily the circumstances could have been reversed; the boy could have held her Stephen as he died. It might still happen in such a way. Her eyes filled at the thought that it might already have.

Albert was watching her carefully as if reading her thoughts. "The one written by Stephen is unsealed," he said, "like maybe Stephen meant for us to read it."

She nodded in agreement and closed her eyes, praying for the boy's mother as her husband read.

"Dear Missus and Mister Johnson,

"By now surely you have heard what happened to your boy at Gettysburg. I was there and met him soon after his regiment climbed the hill at Peach Orchard. He was a brave soldier and did his duty. I pulled him away from battle, and we talked until his time came. He passed peaceful-like while I held him. He spoke highly of you and the little uns at home.

We talked about war and how neither us should of been at Gettysburg that day, how we were just boys and all who should of been home fishing in our creeks. And we weren't the only ones. There were many boys at the battle that day, but they were men by the end of it.

"You would have been proud of Eddie. He died a hero because he did what he had to do.

"I remain yours very sincerely,
"Stephen Ward,
"Massachusetts Ninth Infantry"

Enid met Albert's gaze again and smiled. "Our son's become a man," she said, and her husband nodded in agreement. "A man of honor."

On three occasions, Enid made special trips into town and asked after the family Stephen described: a mother and father with dark-haired twin girls and a younger child, perhaps about five years old. No one seemed to have heard of them, and most suggested they had just been passing through.

Just when she was about to give up, she ran across the parson's wife, Charlotte Brown, at the mercantile, inspecting a length of blue gingham.

"Sounds like Mister and Missus Knight," Charlotte said.

"His name was Lucas, I believe. But I don't remember hers. Anyway, the reverend mentioned them a year or so ago. Had twin girls as cute as buttons, he said, and a younger one, sassy and sweet. Said they'd been involved in a mysterious incident in Utah Territory at a place called Mountain Meadows. Sad business, but he wouldn't tell me what." She picked up a bolt of red calico and held it to the light. "Like this one better?" she asked Enid.

Enid swallowed her impatience and nodded. "A fine piece of cotton," she said. "I believe it will bring out the color in your cheeks."

"Oh, goodness, it's not for me," Charlotte said, but she walked to a long mirror and tucked the edge of the calico under her double chin. She smiled at herself. "But you're right. It is becoming."

"About the Knights…?" Enid stepped to Charlotte's side, meeting her gaze in the mirror.

"The reverend prayed with them. I remember distinctly him telling me about that. They were looking for God's direction… guidance about where to go to raise their children. Give them the best life possible."

Charlotte turned, her eyes suddenly sad. "The little ones weren't children of their flesh and bone, you know. But Lucas and Hannah—yes, I remember now, Missus Knight's name is Hannah—anyway, they had made a promise to the girls' parents, a promise they took more seriously than you can imagine, that they would love the little girls as their own." She paused, nodding slowly. "The reverend was touched by their commitment…to God and to those little orphans."

"Did they tell your husband where they were headed?" Enid was afraid to hope.

Charlotte shook her head in thought. "No, I'm certain the reverend would have told me, and he's never mentioned it. He did say they told him they'd write once they were settled."

"And did they? Write, I mean?"

"I'll ask the reverend. He's off riding circuit just now, but I'll ask him when he gets home." Her eyes were kind as she replaced the bolt of calico and gave Enid her full attention. "Is it important that you find them?"

Enid thought of the hand-carved wooden doll, thinking it was likely whittled by someone who loved the little girls. She nodded. "Yes, it is."

But no letter to the reverend from Lucas and Hannah Knight ever arrived, and after another year of waiting and hoping by Enid, the doll became Lucy's to keep.

Two days after Lucy turned seven, she tucked her doll in a cradle her pa had made for her birthday, then looked up to see a man striding up the hillside.

She frowned, wondering who might come avisiting so early. The sun was barely peeping over the treetops, and the morning birds were still raising Cain as they pecked at ripe, juicy plums in the orchard. Visitors usually waited until after dinner at noon.

Ma wouldn't be happy because Willie and Teddy's chores weren't done, and Thomas wasn't back from market where he'd gone to sell old Sal, the sow.

Lucy reached for her doll and stood, ready to run to tell Mama, when something about the man stopped her in her tracks. She tilted her head and sized him up as he trudged closer.

"Lucy?" he said, squatting down two paces from her.

She nodded, feeling suddenly shy. "Yes sir. That's my name."

He looked down at the doll in her arms, studying it in silence. He didn't ask, but she handed it to him. He smiled as he took it from her and turned it over.

"Right here," he said, his voice soft and low and not at all the way she remembered. "Right here, where this mark is..."

Lucy nodded. She had wondered for the longest time how the dolly's middle got the mark.

"I'll tell you the story sometime, pumpkin." He grinned. "It's a good'n, it is!"

She threw her arms around his neck and squeezed so tight she could feel his Adam's apple bobble up and down. It was then she knew he was crying.

And so was Mama, who'd stepped out to the back porch, watching Stephen when he stood up. "Ma..." he said, looking like he was about to ask something sorrowful and important.

But the question never came. Instead, Stephen ran to Ma's open arms and twirled her around with a joyous shout.

Temecula, California
Summer 1862

Fae skipped along the wooden sidewalk while Ma and Pa shopped in the mercantile. She knew they weren't really her parents, 'cause Meggie and Sarah had told her so. But they were the only ones she could remember. Their real names were Lucas and Hannah, but they liked it when she called them Ma and Pa.

Holding Phoebe close like a real baby, she explained to her doll how they were all starting out on a new adventure. She was careful how she said the word, *ad-ven-ture,* so Phoebe would be sure and understand. Ma and Pa had told them this morning at breakfast that the whole kit and caboodle of them were moving nearer the mountains. Pa wanted lots of land to raise cattle—and lots of babies, he'd told Ma with a wink—the bigger the spread, the better.

Meggie and Sarah were so thrilled they couldn't finish their corn cakes while they talked about raising ponies, just like Pa promised. But Fae had poured lots of honey on hers and ate them right down.

Fae sashayed Phoebe along the sidewalk, just as if the doll were walking on her own. And she made up things for Phoebe to say, then pretended she understood every word.

A stagecoach rattled along the dirt road, catching Fae's attention. "Oh my," she said to Phoebe. "Look at that! It's come for us. We're two big ladies, setting off on an ad–ven–ture today. Where shall we go? How about Sacramento?" It was the only town she knew because Ma and Pa had taken the girls there when they first arrived in California.

With a grown-up sniff, she walked Phoebe to the stage. The driver was busy unhitching the team and didn't notice when Fae opened the door and slipped inside. She giggled and sat straight as a picket in a fence, Phoebe beside her. Then she climbed down and stepped back outside to peer in at Phoebe, taking a trip all by herself.

"Fae!" Meggie yelled from the mercantile. "Come quickly! That's not the right stage. Ours is the next one."

"Hurry!" Sarah called, cupping her mouth with her hands. "Ma and Pa want us to help load!"

Fae ran to her sisters, proud to be strong enough to help. Not until Sarah looked at her in alarm as the stagecoach rattled away did she realize what she'd done.

"Where's Phoebe?" Sarah asked with a puzzled frown.

Fae turned to the stagecoach as it picked up speed, reins jangling and carriage creaking. She ran after it. "Phoebe!" she sobbed. "Come back!"

CHAPTER TWELVE

Eden's Pass, California
1935

Faith Green sat in the Model A outside Secondhand Rose, her gaze again resting on the little soldier still standing beside the toy cannon in the window. Though it was now spring, the weather had turned chilly, causing the tender-hearted quilting ladies in all three sewing circles to work twice as hard on quilts and blankets and children's sweaters. Faith was making her third delivery this week to Anna Rose.

Her friend was rearranging the goods in her front window, and when she saw Faith, she turned the doll to face her and playfully set it hopping along the shelf. They both giggled as the wooden soldier seemed to come to life, marching bravely among the copper pots and teakettles and wooden-handled irons.

Still chuckling, Faith gathered up the newest stacks of blankets, quilts, and clothing. She was especially proud of a small rag quilt her sisters had sewn. A raggedy quilt, they called it, entirely of their own design. They had used flannel, fringed on the edges of each square, each a riot of mismatched blue plaids and bright calico prints.

Anna Rose's face brightened as she held the door open for Faith. "You're an angel," she said, assessing the latest array of goods. "I don't know what I would do without you."

Faith shook her head and held up a hand to stop any further compliments. "It's our Eden's Pass womenfolk who are the angels," she said. "I'm just proud to use the Model A for such a good cause."

Anna Rose bent over the rag quilt. "And this!" A small whistle escaped her lips. "I'd like to see more of these. Can you imagine the little one who will have sweet dreams under this cover? So cuddly warm and secure... What a gift of love." She looked up. "Do you think we can talk the girls into sewing another?"

"I'll ask." Faith knew how pleased they would be to hear of their raggedy quilt's eager reception. They would likely begin another as soon as they could find more brightly colored flannel.

Anna Rose stacked the new quilts near some baskets of yarn while Faith carried the sweaters to the children's clothing table. Then with a smile, she stood back as Anna Rose placed the rag quilt near the toy soldier in the window, dusted off her hands, and stood back, hands on hips, to admire the arrangement. "Look how the colors match. It's as if the little soldier and the raggedy quilt were made for each other."

Faith nodded in agreement. "Doc will be pleased you're saving the little soldier for his return."

"I wouldn't have it any other way. Speaking of Doc"—she patted her apron pocket, then withdrew a wrinkled envelope—"I heard from him just yesterday. Take a look at these postage stamps. This came all the way from São Paulo. Can you imagine such a thing?" She touched the stamps with her fingertips, then again met Faith's gaze. "They've started their lessons at the Portuguese language school. He says they'll soon be leaving by boat for the headwaters of the Amazon."

"I admire him for following God to such a place." She didn't say so, not wanting to worry Anna Rose, but she knew of the dangers they would face. The tribes in the Brazilian rain forests were known to be brutal. She breathed a quick prayer for the young couple's safety.

Anna Rose nodded. "Indeed, it is an adventure. A dangerous one. But listen to this." She pulled the letter from the envelope, adjusted her spectacles, and began to read:

> "We are following God's leading in our lives, so our fear of the unknown is lessened by knowing we're in the center of his hand. A long time ago, my dearest Ivy Magill told me that all journeys, no matter how difficult, and no matter whether they are a journey of the heart or of the feet, begin by first placing your hand in the heavenly Father's. It is he who leads us and determines our paths.
>
> "She also taught me never to give up, no matter what. With a God like ours, who are we to turn tail in fear? He is with us each step of the way."

"Ivy Magill," Faith mused. "What a legacy she left to this young man through her words. I never knew..."

Anna Rose smiled. "I wonder if she ever realized the influence she had on Nate McKenzie's life."

Faith thought about Anna Rose and how her acts of kindness had helped so many, herself included. "I wonder if any of us realize how we might change the direction of someone's life by following the nudges God is giving our hearts."

Faith stopped outside the window, the way she always did when leaving Secondhand Rose, and let her gaze linger on the wooden soldier. Just as it had the first time she saw it, a fleeting, almost aching memory nudged at her heart. And as always, she shook her head in wonder as she walked to the Model A to crank it to a start.

Soon she was shifting and grinding gears and putt-putting along the main road leading from Eden's Pass. How the little town had changed since she first moved here with her family seven decades ago. Then it was mostly ranchos, populated with cattle and vaqueros. Now, it had grown up to be a real town. After Fin died, she moved back to the family home, still in the country, but with considerably less acreage than when her pa had run it as a ranch.

Wisps of her bobbed hair tousled in the wind as she picked up speed and turned the Model A into the barren gold hills. She rounded three curves, crossed a small stone bridge, and turned up the family drive. Soon she arrived at the tall and pretty whitewashed house she shared with her sisters.

The sight of it never failed to lift her spirits, with its green shutters that matched the weeping willows and live oaks out front. Window boxes adorned every sill on both stories with tall, staid geraniums of scarlet, rose, and sunset hues. A wide wraparound porch looked out over a pond that was framed with cattails and marsh grasses and dotted with a family of newly hatched ducklings.

The girls fanned themselves as they rocked side by side on the porch and watched the Model A lurch and hop to a halt. Neither of them looked close to their eighty-four years, not with their jaunty white knots of hair piled atop their heads. Meg even dared to pat rouge on her cheeks from time to time, and Sarah wore lipstick, of all things, a pretty, shiny pink that made her eyes twinkle.

"Baby Fae," Meg called with a smile and a wave of her slender fingers, "where've you been, child?"

Sarah laughed and winked at Faith, knowing how much her sister disliked her childhood name. The girls teased her mercilessly even after all these years. No matter that they were old women now, living on the sunset side of it all. Or on the heaven side of life, as Sarah was prone to say.

Faith made her way up the stairs to the porch and sat down with a heavy sigh in the wicker rocking chair between her sisters. "Where've I been?" She glanced out at the Model A and smoothed her hair, still exhilarated by the drive. "Stopped by Secondhand Rose. Took me longer than I expected."

"How did Anna Rose like our raggedy quilt?" Meg rocked gently in her chair.

"I hope it warms some child's heart," Sarah said. "That counts more than what Anna Rose thinks...though I do like pleasing her, too." She shook her head slowly. "What a saint the woman is, with all she does for the poor."

Faith nodded in agreement. "Every time I stop by, I'm struck by her giving heart." She paused. "She has the dearest little wooden soldier in her front window. I notice it each time I go in the shop. Have I told you about it?" Her sisters shook their heads. "It's wooden. Hand-carved, I expect, likely by someone for a beloved child."

Sarah smiled and exchanged a glance with Meg. "Remember the dolls our papa made for us? Whittled them both."

Remembering, Meg laughed and dabbed at her eyes with the corner of her apron. "I called mine Rosebud."

"And gave her to the little black-eyed Pawnee girl." Sarah smiled at her sister, thinking back on the day. "I was never more proud of you."

"That was after you squealed and tried to grab your Phoebe away from the poor little thing." She laughed. "You were ready to yank her braids right off her head if Papa hadn't come into their camp and grabbed you away."

"Phoebe," Fae mused. "The one you gave to me." She leaned

forward in her rocking chair, studying her sister. "It must have broken your heart to let her go."

"Not so much as when we watched her leave on the stagecoach." Sarah met Faith's eyes, her own still holding the memory of sorrow. "Do you remember how you cried that day?"

"I always wondered what happened," Meg said, "after she rode off in the stagecoach all by herself." Her expression was merry. "Wouldn't it be grand to know?"

"Phoebe might have gone on to the most thrilling adventures we could ever imagine," laughed Sarah. Her eyes seemed to take on a golden glow at the thought.

"Mercy," sighed Faith, leaning back and fixing her gaze on the duck pond, "just think of it." The ducklings chattered softly as they waggled slowly across the pond, and overhead a hawk soared, its tail glinting red in the sunlight.

Still thinking about Phoebe, the doll she'd loved so long ago, Faith glanced up at the bronze plaque Sarah had hung beside the front door. It was high enough to meet the eyes of anyone crossing the threshold, low enough to touch if someone so desired.

And Sarah did just that each time she passed it. Often Faith saw a softness, a glimmer of some distant, precious memory, in her expression as she traced her fingertips over the words:

I HAVE LOVED THEE WITH AN EVERLASTING LOVE:
THEREFORE WITH LOVINGKINDNESS HAVE I DRAWN THEE.

JEREMIAH 31:3

Dear Ones,

What a joy it's been to tell the story of the little wooden doll that captivated me in *The Veil.* She's been nestled in my heart for these past few years, just waiting for her own book. For those who haven't read *The Veil,* let me tell you a bit about this powerful story.

The Veil is based on a historical event. A wagon company from northwest Arkansas, made up of families on their way to California, passed through Utah Territory, not knowing that a warlike frenzy had taken over the territory and its people. The wagon train captain, Alexander Farrington, his wife Ellie, and his twin daughters, Sarah and Meg (portrayed in *Phoebe's* epigraphs), were among those real families in this company. At a deceptively peaceful meadow in the mountains west of Cedar City in September 1857, a renegade group of local militants and the wagon train families came together in an event that shook the nation when the truth was uncovered years later.

An even more compelling reason for returning to Phoebe's story was to continue the thread of God's redemption, grace, and unconditional love that began in *The Veil.* Many who were touched by the characters in *The Veil* have written to ask what happened to the families of the wagon train, especially the children. In *Phoebe,* we see evidence of his ever-present grace continuing through the generations, something that blessed me even as I wrote.

I love hearing from my readers. You can write to me at either of the following addresses:

Diane Noble

P.O. Box 3017

Idyllwild, CA 92549

e-mail: diane@dianenoble.com

And I invite you to stop by my little corner of the Web at www.dianenoble.com.

May the same words that Sarah's pa carved on her beloved doll remain etched in your heart forever, for it's your heavenly Father who has written them there:

I HAVE LOVED THEE WITH AN EVERLASTING LOVE:
THEREFORE WITH LOVINGKINDNESS HAVE I DRAWN THEE.

JEREMIAH 31:3

Blessings,

Diane Noble

Praise for
The Veil

"Prepare to burn the midnight oil. I couldn't put this book down."

—FRANCINE RIVERS

"Diane Noble's thoughtfully paced, can't-put-down narrative is filled with characters I cheered for, cried for, grieved for. Historical research and spiritual insights underpin this stunning work by one of Christian fiction's finest writers."

—LIZ CURTIS HIGGS

"*The Veil* is a fine piece of writing that tells a foreboding and compelling story of power and spiritual searching within the lives of ordinary people."

—JANE KIRKPATRICK

"Noble's work is a tour de force, a compelling story of romance, courage, and enduring love set against a tumultuous backdrop of prejudice and fear."

—RONALD WOOLSEY, author/historian

The Veil is available at your local bookstore.